AF351710

The Catnap Fumblers

book II

SOLICITOUS MISSTEPS

J.B. THWAITE

Napuke Books

Copyright © 2024 by J.B. Thwaite

All rights reserved.

No part of this publication may be reproduced, distributed, or transmitted in any form or by any means without the prior written permission of the publisher, except for the use of brief quotations in a book review.

The story, all names, characters, and incidents portrayed in this production are fictitious. No identification with actual persons (living or deceased), places, buildings, and products is intended or should be inferred.

Ebook: 978-952-7600-03-0

Paperback: 978-952-7600-04-7

Hardcover: 978-952-7600-05-4

Book cover and illustrations: J.B. Thwaite aka Napukettu.

Publisher: Napuke, Finland (http://books.napuke.com)

Content information

Includes themes unsuitable for younger readers.
For a detailed list of potentially upsetting or triggering content, please visit http://books.napuke.com.
There is a helpful glossary and cast of characters at the end of the book.

Lillian Underhall hired
Divorce and second marriage
Vincent disappears
The Calomel Incident
Whitskersey
Làirig Áir
Iris's first treatment
Julian disappears
Justin dies
The ARF study
Julian surrenders
Vincent's cottage burns down
Fire at the ReM Clinic
1858 Vincent (July 1st)
1859 Prototype MOP device
1860
1861
1862
1863 Julian & Justin (April 16th)
1864
1865
1866
1867
Benton House
1868
1869 Rhys (May 5th)
1870
1871
1872
1873
1874
1875
1876 The ReM Clinic
1877 Jonathan (September 30th)
1878 The Bulb Laboratory
1879 Jacob (August 3rd)
1880
1881
Agnes Point
1882
1883 Jasmine (June 9th)
1884 Ren (March 22nd)
1885
1886 The GODS
(The Guardian Observation and Diagnostics System)
1887
1888
1889
1890
1891
1892
1893
1894
1895
1896

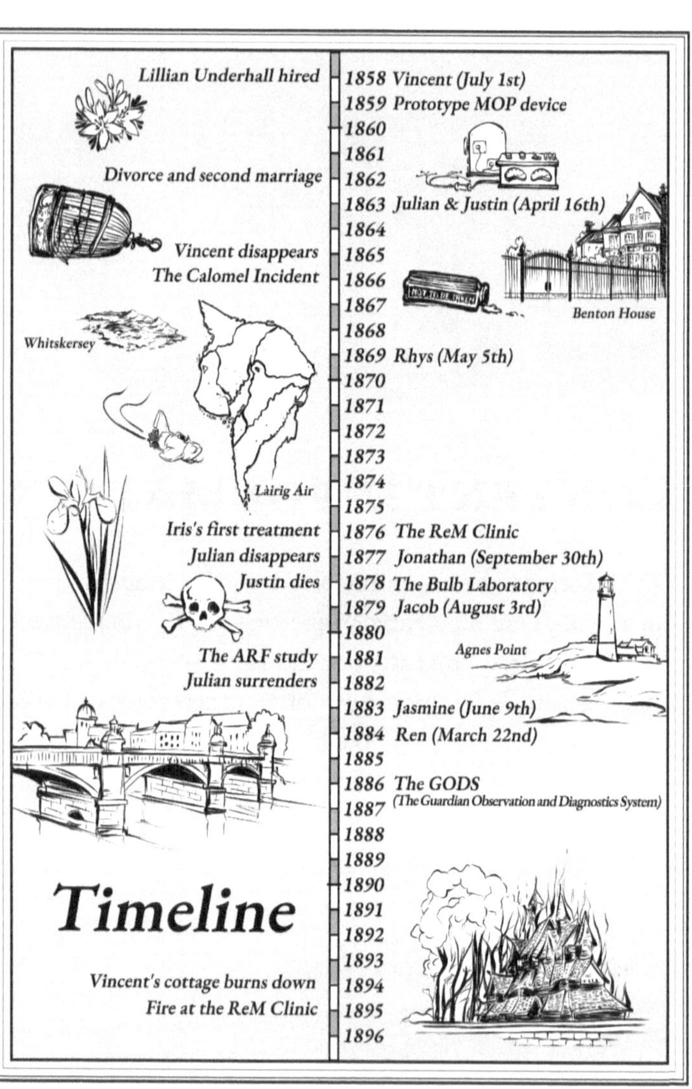

Timeline

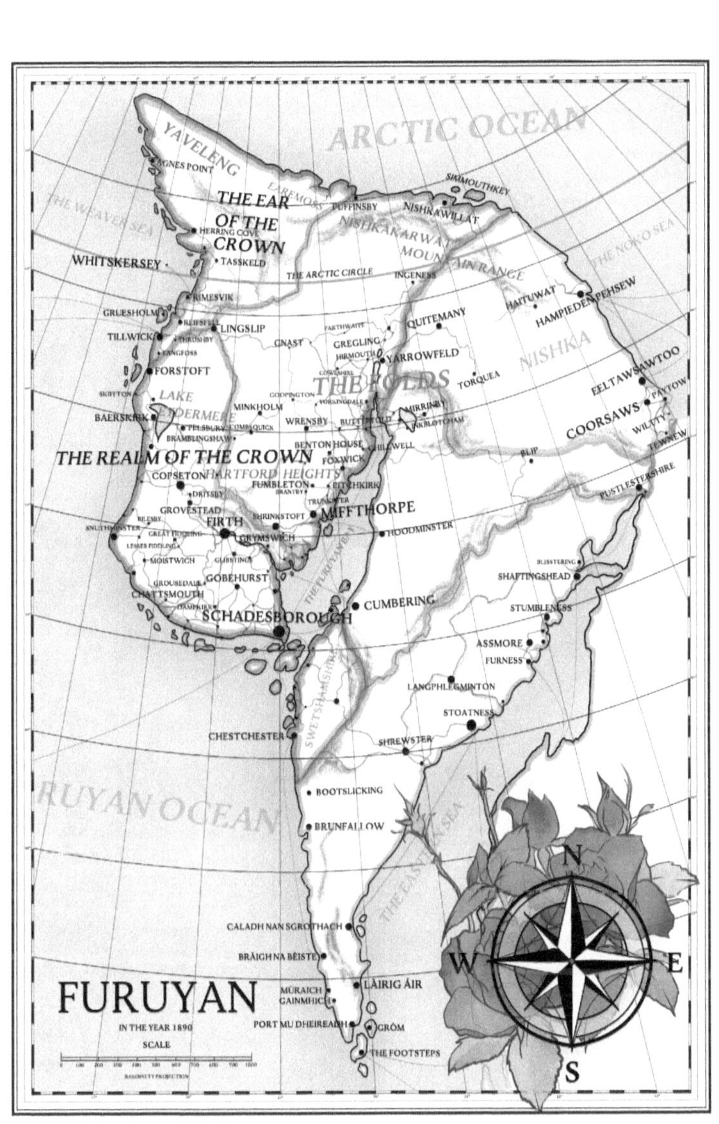

ARCTIC OCEAN
YAVELENG
AGNES POINT
LAREMOSS
THE WEAVER SEA
SIMMOUTHKEY
PUFFINSBY
NISHRAWILLAT
THE EAR OF THE CROWN
HERRING COVE
NISHKAKARWAN MOUNTAIN RANGE
THE NCKO SEA
WHITSKERSEY
TASSKELD
THE ARCTIC CIRCLE
INGENESS
HAITUWAT
HAMPIEDEN PEHSEW
RIMESVIK
QUITEMANY
GRUESHOLM
BEHSELL
LINGSLIP
FARTHWAITE
GREGLING
NISHKA
TILLWICK
THRUSBY
CNAST
HIRMOUTH
YARROWFELD
LANGFOSS
COWEMHILL
TORQUEA
EELTAWSAWTOO
PAYTOW
FORSTOFT
GOOPINGTON
THE FOLDS
WILTYY
SKIBTON
LAKE ENDERMERE
MINKHOLM
YORKINGDALE
MIRRINBY
COORSAWS
TEWNEW
BAERSKIRK
WRENSBY
BUTTERFOLD
INKBLOTOHAM
TILSBURY
COMBSQUICK
CHILWELL
BLIP
TUSTLESTERSHIRE
BRAMBLINGSHAW
BENTON HOUSE
THE REALM OF THE CROWN
FOXWICK
COPSETON
HARTFORD HEIGHTS
FUMBLETON
PITCHKIRK
DRITSBY
BRANTRY
TRUNKSVEA
GROVESTEAD
SHRINKSTOFT
MIFFTHORPE
BLESBY
FIRTH
HOODMINSTER
BLISSTERING
SNUTHMINSTER
GREAT FIDDLING
GRYMSWICH
SHAFTINGSHEAD
LESSER FIDDLING
THE FURUYAN
MOISTWICH
GUBBSTING
STUMBLENESS
GROUSEDALE
GOBEHURST
ASSMORE
CHATTSMOUTH
DAMPKIRK
FURNESS
SCHADESBOROUGH
CUMBERING
LANGPHLEGMINTON
SWETSHAMSHIRE
STOATNESS
CHESTCHESTER
SHREWSTER
RUYAN OCEAN
BOOTSLICKING
BRUNFALLOW
THE EASTERN SEA
CALADH NAN SGROTHACH
N
BRÀIGH NA BÉISTE
LÀIRIG ÁIR
W
E
MÙRAICH GAINMHICH
PORT MU DHEIREADH
GRÒM
FURUYAN
IN THE YEAR 1890
THE FOOTSTEPS
SCALE
S
0   100 200 300 400 500 600 700 800 900 1000
BASGNYETT PROJECTION

Note from the Author

This book is written in British English. Here is a bucket of z's for my American readers to take along and add where you see fit. Take the whole bucket with you, so you can collect all the extra letters (mainly u's) into it. You can return it at the end of your read, and I will take care of the recycling. I ~~apologise~~ apologize for the inconvenience!

Because this story has fairly many points of view and a couple of time jumps, I've added character-specific dinkuses (the decorative thingamabobs) at the start of every chapter and scene break (where the point of view changes) to clue you in.

I am deeply sorry for any typos, extra commas or grammatical mistakes in this book. I and my editor have been on a lengthy expedition to hunt and catch the pesky things, but we are only human, and some may have slipped through. My inbox is always open should you want to point them out to me.

And lastly, I am grateful to anyone willing to give my story a chance. It's something I've been working on for over a decade, so I sincerely hope you enjoy it!

DEDICATIONS

To all the imperfect mothers out there who have made mistakes, regret some of their choices but strive to do better.
To all the people who feel inadequate but keep trying regardless. Be kind to yourself. No one is perfect.

But also, to all the children who feel unloved. It's not your fault that your parents struggle with parenting, trauma or don't know how to express themselves.

CHAPTER 1

June 1857

H osta poured the tea into two cups and squeezed a few drops of lemon into her father's cup. A seed floated to the surface, and she carefully lifted it out with a spoon. A half teaspoon of sugar, a calm stir: a comfortable routine.

Another pesky seed emerged. She fished it out with her pinky and wiped her finger hastily on her skirt. With her skin still crawling, she carried the cups into her father's study, set his cup on the desk next to him and sat in the seat on the opposite side.

Her father—one of the leading scientists in his field of sleep science—was amidst writing something, and Hosta still had her own tasks unfinished, so she picked up her pen and resumed without bothering him.

To prepare her for becoming his full-time assistant, Hosta's father delegated these tasks to her every evening. They were mostly calculations of ratios of the different ingredients and dosages for patients of various constitutions. She would complete them, and he or his current assistant, Walter—a tall and charismatic if somewhat stoic young man—would take a look at them in the morning to make sure she had done them correctly. With such little margins of error, and her only being seventeen, she was glad to be entrusted, even if she still operated under her father's strict and watchful eye.

"Thank you," he acknowledged the teacup that had appeared while he was engrossed in whatever he'd been drafting.

"You're welcome!" Glad that this was often the extent of the niceties they exchanged, Hosta refocused on her calculations in the comfortable silence that ensued.

"Perhaps it is time for you to turn in?" her father suggested an hour later. It seemed he had noticed her coming to the end of the page she was working on.

"All right." She smiled at him, knowing he'd likely interrupted her on purpose. "Thank you."

"You can leave them there. I will have Walter look at them in the morning."

Hosta nodded. She'd managed more pages than usual, and she was fairly sure she'd done a perfect job. She could have continued at this for hours for how soothing it felt, but her father was right. Rest was important.

"Good night," she said and stood up to go.

"Good night, My Sweet."

Hosta woke up, excited. She was even more excited when she bumped into Walter in the corridor and he handed her the previous day's calculations, complimenting her on her speed and efficiency. She knew she was worth every compliment, but him offering them unprompted meant a lot to her. Enough, in fact, that she was tempted to rush to tell her worrywart of a father and risk him realising how smitten she was with his dashing assistant.

She hurried into the kitchen first, though, for a freshly-baked scone and the usual breakfast cups of tea. No extra seed this time. A relief.

Since her father rarely cared for anything on the side, she forwent using a tray, shoved the jam-laden scone into her mouth and grabbed the teacups. Hands thus full when she reached the study door, she used her elbow to knock.

There was no answer.

On any other day, she would have knocked again and waited to be called in, but, too high-strung for manners this morning, she simply could not bear waiting. Despite having to juggle two cups of tea teetering on their saucers, she managed to pry the door open without spilling.

A single shoe lay on the floor next to the stool that had fallen over. Its laces were open. The other shoe was still laced up and on its owner mid-air.

It took her jaw a small moment to unclench enough to let go, but, when it did, the scone rolled to the floor along with whatever else she'd been carrying.

"You swine! You repugnant piece of faecal matter!" Hosta screamed at the corpse hanging from a rafter, as if it held some capacity to hear her if she screamed loudly enough. "What the hell did you do? Why? Why did you do this?!"

In her mouth, the sweetness of the scone soured and blended in with her fury, burning, *searing* through every molecule of her body, thrusting her forth to grab anything she could—a lamp, a stool, a poker from the fireplace, anything left lying on the desk or on the floor—to fling at her father and to beat him until her mother walked into the room and stopped her, barely in time for no one else to see the mess she'd made.

No amount of anger could bring him back, and, at the tail end of it, his betrayal and abandonment stung so badly she didn't care if it had. All her rage was ever good for was making a bloody mess of things, but even knowing that, she could not curb it. Would not curb it. Anything was better than giving up without a fight. Anything.

Because Hosta could not legally inherit her father herself, her father had left his research and business to the assistant, Walter Wakefield, with the condition that he would marry her. It was his way of ensuring she still had a secure future and a roof over her head. Hosta did not care for or appreciate his considerations, but she was pragmatic enough to accept the offered security. Luckily, she was easy enough on the eyes for the assistant to agree to the arrangement without contest, and so, Hosta Aelia soon became Hosta Wakefield.

Now more than ever, Hosta was adamant to follow in her father's footsteps—albeit in profession only. Her father might have not been able to save himself from the Aelia family curse, but she was sure as hell never going to give up without a fight and take her own life on account of it!

July 1858

Hosta had never considered having children, but she was rather smitten with her handsome new husband, who was keen to have someone to eventually leave the business to.

She was much less smitten with him during the pregnancy because the exhaustion and persistent nausea forced her to leave her work and studies earlier than expected, and not being able to do either of those things meant she was mostly cooped up in her house, without the comfort of her usual routines, with nothing to do but try to prepare herself for motherhood.

Walter hadn't exactly ever been a doting husband even before the pregnancy, but because she was young and pretty, he had given Hosta plenty of attention in the bedroom, which she'd assumed meant he cared about her.

Now that she was pregnant, he had initially attempted to give her that same attention, but she was much less interested in his advances due to the exhaustion and urge to vomit from the slightest irritant.

Worried that he might completely lose interest in her, she had tried to withstand the symptoms to please him a time or two, but her body was in too much pain adjusting to the growing baby and preparing for the birth, and he did not find her growing form especially desirable, so, after a few of these attempts, he gave up trying.

Alone in the nursery, Hosta soothed her baby, trying not to succumb to the exhaustion-fuelled panic when he didn't respond to any of her efforts. She tried to stroke his hair and cheek, cuddle him, rock him and sway him gently, but all of those things only made him cry harder. The sound of his cries shredded her insides with each passing second as if there were anything left to shred after weeks of this—ever since his birth. She seemed entirely powerless to save him from the agony of being alive.

The doctor had told her she was incompetent and needed to be more loving and gentle, but perhaps she didn't have that in her, because no matter what she did, he would still scream and wail like this until his small body became incapable of it and finally surrendered to some semblance of sleep for a few precious moments.

According to the doctor, he was a healthy baby boy with nothing whatsoever wrong with him. "Sometimes," the man had said, "a baby can have a slightly weak constitution and cry a little more than usual, but this much is not unheard of, and it will likely right itself in time when you learn to be a better mother."

How much time?

Hosta hushed her baby, her mouth and lips parched but eyes leaking from the pain of knowing she was already weeks deep into failing as a mother.

Because it was her first time and she was a budding scientists' assistant, she had taken pride in finding out everything there was to know about child-rearing by reading every book she could find and interviewing everyone around her who would know anything about it.

She now realised how naïve she had been. Nothing could have prepared her for the disarray and anxiety in her mind as the baby would not latch on properly to feed. When he finally did, it was so painful her teeth felt like they would cave in from her clenching so hard. But she had no choice but to endure, otherwise they would blame her for not even providing sustenance for the poor child.

As baby Vincent kept crying in the middle of the night without mercy, Walter came into the room to scream at her.

"Make that bloody child stop disturbing my sleep this instant! How hard can it be?!"

It was at this moment that something long since fractured shattered within Hosta, and she wondered if she would be released from all this if she gently but firmly twisted the baby's neck—

"Get me a nanny, Walter!" Frightened by her own thoughts, she shrieked at her husband and pushed the baby into his lap. Somebody needed to save this fragile being from her. She was a monster. She was unfit. She would end up killing him if they did not take him to safety.

And no matter how hard she cried, she could not wring out the darkness in her heart.

Hosta sat in the dark. It was where she always went when she went asleep: no light or sound save for her breathing and tired sobs. She could feel herself move if she moved herself, she could tell she was sitting if she sat, but there seemed to be nothing tangible around her. It was as if she were suspended mid-air somewhere, all the way until the hallucinations started.

The hallucinations took a while to start, and today was one of those days that the darkness felt particularly oppressive and merciless. She had handed her baby over to the nanny.

Don't cry.

Hosta jolted from the fright. Not once in her eighteen years of life had she heard a voice in this state.

It's all right. Please don't cry. He's still your baby. You haven't failed if you haven't stopped trying.

"Who are you?" Hosta turned her head but the view remained the same. Something touched her hand, and she jolted again.

You can't see? Don't be afraid. I only want to help. The voice was somewhat flavourless, so it was difficult to tell whether it belonged to a woman or a man, but they sounded kind enough for Hosta to not flinch a third time when someone took her hands and stroked them softly. *I think there might be something wrong with the baby, though.*

"The doctor said—"

How long did he examine him for? What does he really know? You're his mother. I know you feel there's something wrong, in here. Whoever it was lifted Hosta's hands to press them against her chest. *We both know something is not right. You're a smart woman. You will figure this out.*

"But how? I don't even know where to start!"

You start from the beginning, silly. I will help you. I have some access to him through here. It's not much, but I can tell there's something wrong. Just like you're not able to see, I wonder if he's also alone in the dark.

"Surely darkness is nothing for a baby to be afraid of?"

Isn't it the first time he's experiencing it alone? And you are there, but his experience of you is your warmth and heartbeat from inside the womb. I think whatever it is that's wrong with him is preventing him from settling down enough to recognise you.

"I don't know who you are, but thank you. I will look into it."

I'm just someone who admires you. Remember, you haven't failed unless you give up. The owner of the voice squeezed her hands.

Hosta wasn't yet ready to believe the words but accepted the kindness and encouragement. If she couldn't soothe her son, perhaps there was still something she could do for him as a scientist?

Chapter 2

December 1895

Hosta woke up in an unfamiliar house, but what made this even more troubling, was the manner with which she was woken up: by a man pulling her along by her clothes, dragging her across the room.

"Keep an eye on her," she heard someone say.

She screamed.

"Shit, this woman—!" A hand was placed on her mouth. Despite making every effort to struggle, she was tied and gagged. She couldn't make sense of what was happening, but the sounds she heard were fueling her imagination.

"Take her to safety. I can manage." An absolute giant of a man grabbed her and carried her down to the bottom floor of the house.

"Hide in here, and do not come out until I come get you," the man said.

"Wait! Where's my baby? Oh my God, where's my baby?" She reached at him, begging for an answer.

"There is no baby. Stay here!" He shook her away and left her in the small washroom.

No baby? What do you mean, there's no baby? What had happened to her precious baby?! The door was slammed shut in her face, and she was too frightened to open it and follow the man.

Where was Walter? He wasn't up there somewhere, was he? None of the voices had sounded familiar. The noises coming from the other side of the door made her cower at the far end of the confined space, in darkness, trying to suppress her panicked wails to not attract attention.

Had someone drugged her and brought her here. Had they taken her baby?

But why?

December 1895

After what seemed like hours, the noise died down. There was no sign of the giant who had promised to come get her. She took deep breaths in hopes of finding enough calm to stop crying, but when a man covered in blood opened the washroom door, she was again overcome by her instinct to scream.

Again, her mouth was covered, and she was pulled from the washroom by the same man who had dragged her across the room before. They tied her up, hooked her to a machine and injected her with something. Perhaps it was a blessing to lose her senses and her consciousness, because she was at the limit of her tolerance.

December 1895

When Hosta came to, the house was quiet. She lay on a sofa, unsure whether she'd just had a nightmare or whether she was yet to wake up from one.

She was still alive.

Why would they leave her after all that if it hadn't been a dream? Why did she feel like she was supposed to have a baby? Wasn't she much too young to be having one?

She sat up. The room she was in was trashed. There were suspicious stains across the floor and a piece of paper left on the table next to her.

You should probably leave as soon as you read this.
For your own good.

She stared at it, hoping for there to be more. Why couldn't there have been a few more words? Something to explain this situation, something to mention where this was, or who she was, for that matter.

She stood up. Her body appeared uninjured, but why was there what seemed like blood on her clothes? The house around her was in pieces. She probably needed to leave, but something compelled her to walk to the stairs.

That room at the top. Why had she been up there? Why couldn't she remember? Had she had a baby? Why did she feel like she was supposed to have a sweet, little baby boy, when she could not recall giving birth?

She took a step up, testing whether the stairs would hold her weight. She would take a look and leave, if for no other reason than to be sure there were no clues left behind for her here.

She climbed up to the first floor. It was in an even worse shape than the ground floor. There wasn't much left of the furniture, and the traces of blood were more widely spread and apparent here.

Was there someone up there still, or had they all left? With the house this quiet, it seemed likely she was here by herself. Embraved by the thought, she climbed the last flight of stairs.

The attic was cool. With the floor littered with broken glass, and her wearing only socks, she searched for somewhere to step, until there was nowhere she could safely set foot. The floor felt sticky and wet under her feet. She looked up.

Dead bodies.

She fell back in fright and scrambled out of the room as quickly as her legs could take her. She nearly fell in the stairs but kept going, running all the way outside.

Snow?!

She slowed her steps in dismay and touched it with her hands. It was snow. How was there snow? She waded through in disbelief, accepting it only when her feet started to feel numb from the cold. And where the hell was this? It was too dark to tell.

Something about her hands didn't look right, even in this light. Why were they so wrinkly? She tried to feel her skin, and it felt rough and foreign. Her fingers on her face traced an unfamiliar surface. Had she burnt herself? But it didn't hurt, so... she would deal with it later.

Where was she supposed to go now? She waded across the yard. She would freeze to death with not enough clothes on, but returning into that house in case someone really was after her didn't seem like an option.

"Excuse me?" A woman's voice called out to her. "Hosta? What are you doing here?"

"You know me?" Hosta looked up to see who it was, but all she could make out in this light was that the woman's posture didn't seem threatening. A friend?

"What on earth has happened to you?" The older woman wrapped her cardigan over Hosta's shoulders. She seemed worried about her. Perhaps she was trustworthy?

"I don't know. There was a note." Hosta tried to give the woman the piece of paper she'd found, but she didn't seem interested.

"Let's get you inside before you freeze. Where's Mr Craft?" the woman asked and guided Hosta down some steps into a basement or a cellar.

The place was warm but didn't seem like anyone's house. In this light, Hosta could finally see who was helping her, but it was no one she could remember ever meeting before. The woman had slightly curly copper hair and a face full of freckles that made her look common. Had she been one of the teachers at Hosta's school, the students would have teased her ruthlessly for looking so unrefined. Even her outfit looked bizarre.

"Who?" Hosta asked. Perhaps this woman had mistaken her for somebody else? But she'd clearly said 'Hosta', hadn't she? And now that she'd been reminded of it, that was her name, wasn't it?

"Was there a man with you when you woke up? What happened to him? What do you remember? How old are you?"

"There were several." Hosta offered the piece of paper again. "But it seems like it might have been a dream. I dreamt I had a baby... but

I'm only sixteen." She glanced at her disgustingly wrinkly hands and hid them behind her back.

"I'd like to help you remember everything." The woman offered Hosta a cup of tea.

"How do I know it wasn't you that made me this wrinkly and old?" Perhaps she was in cahoots with those people from before. Did she really think she would catch her off guard so easily?

"I can do a lot, but that is out of my scope," the woman replied.

"How do I know I can trust you?" Hosta pulled out the little knife she always carried on her to scare off the school bullies, momentarily confused that it had changed shape and size since she'd last seen it and now felt oddly clumsy to hold. She didn't care to wonder why, though, because she was still quick enough to press it to the woman's throat.

"Would it help if I gave you a solid reason for my help? One that is not some bullshit about doing it from the goodness of my heart?" The stranger seemed unrattled. Hosta was irked by her unfazed demeanour but pulled back the knife somewhat.

"What is it?"

"There's a piece of information I need, and it's in there somewhere, sealed away inside your head. That's all I want. I'll help you in whatever way you choose so long as you let me retrieve that. Deal?"

What information could there be that could be relevant for this woman? All Hosta knew was her schooling and what her father had taught her about sleep science, so what use would this woman have with any of it? The proposal sounded suspicious, but considering the circumstances, what else was there to do than hear her out?

"You could do that? You can help?"

"They've put a nasty seal in there. I'll help you remove it. What you do beyond that is your business, but I need you to promise me you'll tell me what you did to Vincent and how to reverse it."

"I don't even know anyone by that name."

"It might be stored as subject one in there, and, if you think you're sixteen, it hasn't happened to you yet.

"I know. I'm not stupid." But the thought of her not being sixteen was incredibly frightening. How old was she? How many years had she lost?

"In any case, you know I wouldn't hurt you because you have what I need. How about you hand me the knife?" the woman bargained. She really seemed to think Hosta was a complete idiot.

"And be left completely defenceless? Are you crazy?" Hosta tightened her grip on the knife.

The woman moved the knife blade aside and started cleaning up the remnants of a teacup off the floor. Hosta hadn't realised something had fallen. Were her ears playing tricks on her? Why were her senses so dull? Why did her body not feel as strong or move as easily as she was used to?

"You seem confident and trustworthy, but you don't know what we are dealing with. There were corpses in that house! They'd fought over something. I need to figure out what that was and why I was there. Judging by that note, I may be in grave danger." Hosta needed to see the damage herself. Did her face look as wrinkly as her hands? Her hair seemed thin and wiry, but it could have been because it was wet. How old was she exactly? Older than her grandmother? "Do you have a mirror somewhere?"

"I may have one in my office."

"What's your name? What do I call you?" She took off the woman's cardigan and used it to dry her hair to see whether it was indeed in such dire state.

"I'm Vera." The woman set the shards of the teacup on the table and took the cardigan Hosta gave back to her. "Follow me."

"What is that?"

The woman held up a worryingly large needle and syringe. It looked different than any Hosta had ever seen, and while she wasn't a nurse, she had seen plenty of medical equipment during her short stint as her father's assistant.

"This is to facilitate the connection between you and the diagnostic equipment. You developed this yourself. I would show you the details, but we haven't got the time for it," Vera explained. She was preparing the equipment in question and looked to be fairly familiar with it.

"You mean to stick me with that thing? And you assume I will let you?"

"Do you want me to help you or not?"

Hosta glanced at the door. Nothing out there made any more sense than this did. Someone was likely after her, and nowhere was safe. If this allowed her to regain some of her memories, perhaps she would stand a chance...?

"This is your handwriting, isn't it?" Vera showed her some notes from a notebook. The content was unfamiliar but the handwriting was indeed hers. That didn't mean someone couldn't have forged it, but flipping through the thing, it would have been a lot of work just to convince her. "I'm following your own instructions for this treatment. You're my only hope. I swear I would not jeopardise my chances with anything unsafe or suspect."

No doubt she thought she was providing Hosta with something she could trust, but this only opened up new doubts and questions. Yet, being faced with this situation alone and admittedly somewhat frightened, Hosta longed for someone she could trust. This copper-curled woman may not have filled all her criteria of trustworthiness, but there was no other help on offer.

"Are there side-effects?"

"Not to my knowledge. I have given this treatment to other patients without issues."

"Will it hurt? Not that I'm scared of pain. I just want to be prepared for it."

"It will sting for sure, but you won't die from it."

"Good." Hosta clenched her jaw, looked away and braced herself.

No sooner than when Lilya Unenhalti had been taken in by her benefactor in Grovestead and they had coached her out of her accent, clothed her in more suitable attire and erased the rest of what was left of her deeply Taka-Nishkan background by changing her name to Lillian Underhall, had she secured a position as the nanny at the house of a local scientist.

It was a moderately wealthy household of a young couple with a newborn. Lillian knocked on the door and was let in by the house-keeper.

The houses around here all looked the same to Lillian, and this one, too, felt a little too rigid and fanciful to her liking: like a box of trinkets too heavy to carry around. The only difference to every other house in the neighbourhood was that this one had the continuous noise of a baby wailing in the background.

There was a small room for Lillian to settle upstairs in the attic, right above the nursery. Soon after she had carried her things up there, the housekeeper took her to meet the baby.

Lillian had several younger sisters and a brother as well as small cousins she had taken care of, but none had been quite as fussy as this one. She did, however, manage to quiet the baby by rocking him to the beat of an old folk song, although the baby would be no closer to sleep despite his silence.

On that first day, when she had finally managed to calm the boy for the first time, only two minutes after silence had descended, the door of the nursery swung open and a woman with black hair and sharp features burst in without knocking.

"Is he all right? What happened?" She rushed to see the baby.

"He's fine…" was all Lillian could think to say. It wasn't so much the abruptness of the woman barging in that had startled her as it was the curve of the woman's mouth, the depth of her eyes, her slender fingers as she reached for her baby, and the sheer impact of her presence in such close proximity.

Lillian held her breath, unable to take her eyes off of the woman. In all her twenty years of age, she had never seen anyone so striking. She helped the woman take the baby in her arms, and the boy started to cry almost immediately.

"Oh, please don't cry…" The woman's unusually animate eyebrows twisted as she tried to coo to the baby. For a brief instant, it looked like she might cry.

The baby's cry only worsened, so she gave the baby back to Lillian, her momentarily gentle features marred by annoyance and then steeled back to indifference.

"You must be the new nanny," she said, lips forming a tight line as she eyed Lillian.

Lillian hushed the baby and resumed rocking until he settled again.

"Lillian Underhall, madam." She curtsied.

"I'm Hosta Wakefield. Thank you for accepting the position." The woman seemed to want to say something more, but after a moment of silence, left without saying another word.

Once the door shut, Lillian gasped for breath.

Holy Äiyä, Akka, the Lowest Earthenfolk and everything in between, that woman was gorgeous! She steadied herself.

These people of the south tended to be dainty and soft, so such strikingly harsh features had taken Lillian completely by surprise. And what an inconvenient moment to be swooning over someone's beauty!

She paced around the room, rocking the baby in her lap, distraught. This was the lady of the house! The mother of the wee baby! Never had she ever felt that struck by someone merely entering the room. What an awful experience!

At least the baby was no longer crying, although he seemed to be watching her disapprovingly.

What a silly notion.

Such a small baby had no conception of propriety nor understanding of the world. Yet, the boy seemed to be looking at her with disdain. He did not look much like her mother, save for perhaps the eyebrows. Was this more his father's disapproving gaze directed at her, for so rudely ogling his wife?

M r Wakefield didn't spend much time in the house because of the noise the baby made. Mrs Wakefield had withdrawn into a room at the back of the first floor, and when Lillian occasionally needed to go ask her to nurse the baby, she seemed amidst something important.

Lillian had never seen a woman immersed in such work before, and having to interrupt her felt just as unpleasant every time.

Mrs Wakefield would order Lillian out of the room while she nursed, and she would look curiously drained and agitated when she called Lillian back to get the baby. Each time, the baby started crying the moment he stopped suckling. Lillian could tell by the sound that she was about to be called back in from the hallway where she'd been waiting.

The oppressive air in the house seemed to only get worse as the weeks went by. It was straining even for Lillian to keep the baby satisfied as she slowly became more sleep-deprived from having to get up repeatedly in the middle of the night.

Mrs Wakefield had left the baby's care all up to Lillian during the day, but she would always turn up to take care of her son during the night and sleep fitfully for perhaps an hour or two in a chair in the nursery.

She was now too tired to order Lillian out of the room during the nightly feeds, so on a few of these occasions, Lillian saw just how cumbersome and painful it was for her to nurse. On a particularly tiresome night, she would let Lillian help hold the baby so that he could latch better.

The shape of her nipples wasn't optimal, but it also shouldn't have caused this much trouble. It seemed the baby was often too tired and lethargic to suckle properly and would drop his hold so often that all of that irritation was making his mother's nipples sore. There was also always a sense of urgency to get him to latch back on before he started to cry, because if that happened and he hadn't yet fed enough, the struggle would worsen by tenfold.

Because no one else was privy to the full extent of the struggle, the people around Mrs Wakefield—the doctors, their housekeeper, the few visiting friends or family members—would offer no help and wave it all away as if it were nothing out of the ordinary. It wasn't

Lillian's place to correct them, but she was enormously tempted more than once to tell a few of these people off. Unfortunately, Mrs Wakefield, despite her otherwise strong no-nonsense exterior, never seemed to voice more than a feeble complaint when her worries were so ruthlessly shot down.

August 1858

"I don't know what to do," Hosta spoke into the darkness in hopes someone would reply. "I try to calm him down, but he doesn't seem to accept any of my affection. The nanny seems far better suited to take care of him."

Thankfully, after a few moments, the voice that had guided her through the worst of her distress the weeks before responded.

He is still your son. Give it some time.

"Do you think he might accept me if I can fix him somehow?" Her question was followed by a lengthy silence. "I have plenty of time for it now. Walter no longer seems interested in me, and the nanny takes care of the baby whenever I'm not nursing. Honestly, I wonder if I should stop that altogether and let Walter hire a wetnurse instead."

You are doing an invaluable job nursing the boy yourself. He will respond to you more favourably if you keep doing it.

"Ah, I know…" Hosta sighed. Would it hurt to say it out loud? What harm could it do? This voice in her head seemed too compassionate to be nothing but a figment of her imagination, and as such, it wasn't as if they would tell anyone. "It's painful. He's so slow. Sometimes I bleed. He doesn't latch on properly, so I'm forced to contort myself into uncomfortable positions for so many hours every day my muscles and joints ache. It feels like he is breaking me down every day, little by little, but my mother says I need to get used to it and bear it. Had I known it would be like this, I wouldn't have had him."

I'm sorry you feel that way.

"It's not like I hate him! I just don't know who that is! Why am I letting him tear me down like this? I know he came out of me, but I don't even know him!"

The voice did not respond. Perhaps they were as appalled by her as she was. How could a mother not adore her son? Poor baby, to have been born from someone like her. "I'm sorry. I don't mean that. I care. Of course I love him. Of course I do. What kind of a mother would I be if I didn't?" She buried her face in her hands even though no one could see her cry in this darkness, and it shouldn't have mattered.

Something soft touched the side of Hosta's face. She looked up from her hands, hoping she could have seen the face somewhere in front of her.

Oh, Love, it's all right to have regrets. It's all right to be sad. You don't have to love him right now. You'll learn in time as you grow to know him. And you're taking care of him, aren't you? You're there for him. Once you get to know him, you'll understand, in your heart, what it was for.

Hosta swallowed, but the tears kept coming.

"Promise?" She desperately needed something to grab on to, a future to look forward to.

It could take a while, but you'll get there. You already care enough to be worried about him. A hand wiped off some of her tears.

"It's because I'm forced to. Walter would kick me out of the house if I didn't! My mother would never speak to me!"

You know that's not true.

"It's true! I'd leave this second if I had the means!" she cried out. "Sometimes I wish I could jump off the Great Grove Bridge—!" Her heart jumped from her own words. No. She clenched her teeth. "I won't."

Don't— Don't say such things. The always so calm and calming voice sounded rattled now. Warm hands took a hold of her hands to hold them tightly. *I promise it will get better. I'm here, and I won't leave you. We'll get through this together.*

Perhaps this was her subconscious telling her the words she'd longed to hear her mother say when she'd tried to confide in her? Only she hadn't dared to voice a quarter of what she'd just told the darkness.

You can do it out of obligation for now. That's admirable. It shows your character. You will learn to do it out of love when you're ready.

"Will you stay with me until then?"

Yes. I'll stay for as long as you need me.

Have you heard of the ancestors?

"I'm asleep?" That meant the boy must have settled for the room to be quiet enough for her to fall asleep. Unless perhaps the nanny had taken him? Good. Hosta was particularly exhausted today. Apparently, so much so that she had fallen asleep while breastfeeding.

Have you heard of the Ancestors? Of the Guardian? the voice repeated.

"Only in passing. How so?"

I can connect to the Guardian. I cannot see your son.

"What does that mean?"

I have access to you, but I cannot connect to your son. It's like he's not there. When he does show up, the connection keeps getting reset, and when I do connect, the latency is atrociously high. The system reports the access marker is invalid.

That made even less sense.

"Could you repeat that in a language I can understand? I'm not sure I speak what you're speaking."

Therein lies the issue. I wish I had the answers for you, but I can only report what I see in the logs for the GateKeeper module. Either the marker is invalid or there's a malfunction in the module itself. I suggest you get your hands on the documentation, on any text you can find about the Guardian, and read it with a critical mind. Your best bet is to find any of the nomadic tribes beyond the Folds where lore and traditions have been passed down and preserved with less contamination from the outside world. The Ancestors might guide you better than I can.

Mrs Wakefield had received a large parcel a week earlier. It didn't change much about her routine of confining herself into her study, but the room quickly became more cluttered and disorganised, and books and paper began to pile on all available surfaces.

On this particular afternoon, she was deep in conversation with the local pharmacist, and the two of them, after lengthy negotiations, seemed to come to an agreement. Later that evening, Mrs Wakefield entered the nursery to breastfeed and asked Lillian to help with the new medicine she had received.

"Please let me know immediately if there are any issues or changes to the current routine." Mrs Wakefield handed the baby over to Lillian. She seemed distracted and eager to get back to whatever she was doing in her room, so Lillian merely nodded and curtsied.

About twenty minutes after Mrs Wakefield had left, the baby fell asleep. Lillian remained worried at first, guarding the boy's breathing like a hawk, wanting to make sure there were no interruptions in its steady pattern.

At the thirty-minute mark, the baby was still asleep. The most Lillian had seen him sleep in one go was for about an hour, so thirty minutes wasn't yet a record. Usually, he had to be held for him to stay asleep, though, so Lillian would wrap him in a sling to ease the load. Now he'd continued to sleep even when Lillian had placed him into his crib.

Vincent slept for three whole hours before he woke up to request attention. Mrs Wakefield came up to feed him, and the boy slept another hour in his mother's arms when she'd dozed off midway.

Lillian watched the two of them, and her heart ached. Mrs Wakefield looked tired and so stretched thin, it seemed like she might just split into pieces and be whisked away by a gust. Anything Lillian could do to help seemed laughably insufficient, but when no one else seemed to care, she vowed to do her best.

The theme of the past three weeks had been money. The baby had slept better than before, but he still hadn't slept for more than three hours at a time, and those three hours came at a hefty price. Mr Wakefield was volubly unhappy about the rapidly depleting finances while Mrs Wakefield tried to assure him the expenses were necessary until she could find a better solution.

As they yelled at each other, their voices carried through every wall of the house, and, with their at times quite colourful language, their arguments were not something one wished for a baby to hear—especially since, with a few hours of sleep now under his belt, said baby had become much more inquisitive about the world around him.

Lillian covered Vincent's ears and swayed him back and forth gently in the sling until he started to show signs of hunger. As soon as the ruckus finally died down, she carried him downstairs to his mother in the back room.

On her way back, Lillian couldn't help but hear some rambunctious laughter from the study near the stairs.

"The woman is mad!" Mr Wakefield was saying. "I'm cutting her off before she makes a pauper out of me."

"How did you even get saddled with someone like her? Can she not handle a single baby? How unfit is she exactly?" Mr Wakefield's companion asked in response.

"It was in the old man's will. Had I known it would turn out like this, I never would have agreed. The only thing she's good for is to serve as decoration, and these days, she's neglected herself to such an extent, she even fails at that."

"What a predicament. Can't say I envy you."

"Oh, but Mr Murray, you forget how weak-minded these people are. I dealt with her father. I'll deal with her as well. All it requires is the right kind of encouragement."

As their conversation turned to other things, Lillian's mind could not rest from the deep unease. There had to be something she could do to guard Mrs Wakefield from her deranged and now vengeful husband.

For someone in Lillian's position, the only effective measure available was distraction. She quickly became an expert at it, keeping him busy and placated with favours in the bedroom.

It was not a pleasant solution, but as long as it served its purpose, Lillian did not mind. After all, she was Nishkan, and she had never built her self-worth on something as trivial as chastity. The inconvenience was usually short lived as Mr Wakefield would last mere minutes before he was spent and sated. An added small chore to keep the peace did not seem at all unreasonable.

"Are you there? I found something today!" Hosta had been looking for a suitable opening for a nap to consult the voice about the ancestors and the documentation, but it seemed that quite often she was left to her own devices with no one replying to her.

I'm here.

"Yes! Good!" Today seemed lucky. "I found a scroll that mentions an archive within the Guardian for storing dreams and memories. Do you know about it?"

Yes, the Guardian collects dream data into an archive for diagnostic purposes.

"The text mentions access for not just retrieving but—!"

Yes, the Guardian is also used for occasionally removing dreams and memories that are harmful for health. The function is not rec-

ommended for frequent use because it's something called 'beta' and it requires what's called 'developer' credentials.

"I need to find a way to use it."

Why?

"For Vincent, of course! He's getting more and more frightened by the needles and treatments, and it's getting so bad that he sometimes won't let me do them. If I could make him forget in between, that would make this so much easier for me."

I see. That does sound beneficial for the both of you. It must be so frightening to not understand what all of it is for. I'm going to see what I can do.

"If you could help me set it up so that I don't need your help for it, that would be for the best. It's been so difficult to get a hold of you lately."

The voice stayed silent for a moment before it responded, *I understand. I will see if I can somehow grant you access through a Manual Override Panel, if you can make one. I have rudimentary instructions here for it, but you might have to search for—*

"Documentation?" It always seemed to boil down to finding the right documentation.

Documentation, yes, and the schematics.

More things to try to unearth, but it would be worth it if it meant Vincent became less fussy.

CHAPTER 5

March 1859

Vincent had finally fallen asleep, and shortly after, Hosta had been unable to keep her eyes open. She really couldn't afford to sleep, but when the darkness enveloped her, it wasn't as if she had a choice.

What's wrong?

"I can't be wasting time sleeping. I have to calibrate the MOP—" Hosta sat up straight out of habit in the presence of company.

You need to rest in order to work. It's fine. You're almost done with the device. I still need a little more time to locate the correct port. The boy is asleep. Enjoy it until he wakes up again.

"How am I supposed to—?" Shoulders too tight to relax, Hosta clutched her skirt to distract herself with the unpleasant, slightly coarse texture of the fabric. After kneading it for a moment, she shook her hands to be rid of the sensation.

I'll help you if that's all right?

"How? Uh—!" Hosta yelped and ducked away from the hands that had touched her shoulders.

I'm sorry. Did I startle you? It's just a massage if you'll let me. The hands rested lightly on Hosta's shoulders again. She turned around to try to feel who was there, but the hands on her shoulders lifted away, and there was nothing where she could reach. *Please just sit down and make yourself comfortable. I won't do it if you don't want me to.*

She didn't know who the voice was or whether they were even a real person, but for a moment there, Hosta had imagined those hands wrapping around her throat to strangle her—deservedly. For another moment, she wondered if that would have been a merciful release from this existence... But then the sight of her father dangling from a rafter like a Midwinter ornament came back to mind, crisp as day.

"So long as you don't try to strangle me," she said between clenched teeth and sat back to where she'd been sitting. No matter how tempting, giving up was never going to be an option.

I would never. The hands rested on her shoulders until she was accustomed to their weight. When they moved, they gently worked to warm up her muscles and, little by little, applied pressure to release the tension.

At first, the sensation of someone touching her proved almost overwhelmingly unpleasant, but as Hosta slowly got used to it and her neck and shoulders finally relaxed, she almost forgot that she wasn't alone.

When the fingers made their way through her hair to rub her scalp, easing her persistent headache, she let out a quiet but deeply satisfied groan. She leaned back without realising, and someone caught her and lowered her carefully onto the floor before continuing.

"This feels nice," she gave a compliment so that whoever it was wouldn't stop. As she relaxed, the fingers gradually eased their pressure until the soft tugging feeling suddenly sent shivers down her spine, startling her.

What is it? the voice whispered.

"I—" The fingers moved again, causing her scalp and neck to tingle until another wave of shivers scurried through her body.

Is it nice?

She strained to see. This time, when she reached up, her fingers met with something smooth. A cheek? "Are you really there?"

I'm here.

"Who are you?"

Something touched her lips. At first, she thought it was the fingers shushing her question, but then she felt a warm breath against her lips.

It doesn't matter. The hands guided Hosta's face so that their lips met full on.

"It matters to me." However, when she said it and opened her eyes, she could see again. Vincent was crying.

If it had had to be a dream, the least it could have been was a little longer.

The light on the device blinked. Hosta consulted the 'documentation' to determine whether the sequence was correct. Because she knew nothing about anything electrical, she'd used every penny she'd scraped up to hire an inventor up in Copseton to build her this device, but so far she hadn't managed to calibrate it well enough for it to connect to the Guardian.

The ancestors had been much too cryptic, leaving out key details from their documentation. Perhaps this wasn't the correct documentation at all? Her agent had reportedly procured it from some shady old man in Ingeness. It didn't exactly sound like a reputable source.

The light still blinked in a steady succession.

Vincent was asleep in the sling that the nanny was wearing. Walter had refused to pay for Vincent's medicine, so the boy was back to only sleeping an hour or so at a time. Because of the treatments, he had been increasingly difficult to pacify while awake. The nanny had certainly had her hands full with him and would deservedly try to catch any opportunity to nap when the baby finally slept for a moment. Hence she, too, had fallen asleep an hour earlier.

Was this blink rate different from the last? Hosta measured the beats. Was it different enough for it to be worth catching some sleep to consult the voice? The voice had been trying to catch the signal from their end for days to no avail.

Having stayed up most of the night, Hosta was too tired to trust her eyes, and she was further tempted to sleep because it would give her an opportunity to catch some much-needed rest. Each time was risky, though, because she wouldn't wake up before being woken up—usually by Vincent screaming—and that meant she would likely need to nurse... All of this meant more time away from calibrating the device.

Hosta moved aside the top hem of the sling to check that the connectors were still securely in place on Vincent's head. She also double-checked the wiring and stared tiredly at the blinking light.

It must have been a little different from the last three rates at least? If she stared for long enough, it seemed like it would occasionally blink a brief off-beat sequence.

A short nap would help her to determine whether she was just too sleep-deprived to see right... She lowered her head to lean on the desk. At this point, any surface was fine. Her head was buzzing quietly from her being so tired.

Only a moment later, everything became pitch black.

Is it doing it? Is it? Hosta? Hosta? The voice sounded frantic.

"That's what I was going to ask you..." Hosta made an effort to shake off her exhaustion—with not much success.

It gave me a file transfer notification five minutes ago when I tried to send the patch through port 6698. The Pangolin Attachment Protocol was triggered, but there's nothing useful in the logs that would have explained why. It looks like it might have worked. Is he still asleep? Did the light start blinking more rapidly a moment ago?

"I may have seen it flicker, but I'm too tired to trust my eyes."

I'm going to send you a wake up signal, and when you wake up, see if it flickers some more. I'll send the suggested updates through, and that should stabilise the connection. If it stabilises, the light should remain steadily on after the install. OK?

"All right..." There was a 'wake up signal'? That seemed convenient but also loathsome.

Hosta had been following advice similar to this throughout this project, and, although she couldn't quite understand half of what the voice was saying, the voice sounding this excited must have been a good sign.

The rough surface of the desk against her cheek alerted Hosta that she was awake. She needed to pull herself together... But the light was blinking slowly again.

She'd been staring at it blink at this rate for days, so she was filled with dread, thinking perhaps it had been a dream.

It kept blinking.

After it had been blinking like this for twenty minutes, Hosta consulted the documentation, even if she'd already read those passages countless times before.

"The MOP device is in pairing mode when the indicator light blinks slowly. If you are having issues with establishing the connection, reset the device by pressing the reset button for 5 seconds and consult the user manual."

Having upturned every rock south from Lingslip, Hosta's agent had produced but two people who'd even heard of the 'documentation' for a MOP device, and neither of them were familiar enough with it to know of a 'user manual'. There was no one to consult.

Hosta could only thank her luck that she'd been too tired to truly get excited, because it seemed the device still hadn't been able to calibrate itself, and no 'updates' had been 'sent through'. She wiped her tears and got back to deciphering the 'troubleshooting' passages.

Three days and hundreds of minute adjustments later, Hosta flicked the device off and back on again to see the indicator light blink through the 'boot sequence' as well as a completely novel rapid sequence of blinks.

The blinking continued like this for several minutes until it stopped with the light steadily on.

"Finally?!" Hosta yelled before she thought to stop herself.

The nanny, who had again fallen asleep with the baby in her sling, was roused from her sleep in the armchair.

"What is it?" she whispered.

"It worked? I think it worked! It must have worked, right?" Hosta stared at the light as unblinking as it was. Then she glanced at the nanny, surprised to see the woman tearing up.

But why, when even Walter didn't care a rodent's bottom about this baby? Ms Underhall was nothing but hired help, not compensated nearly enough for the gruelling months she'd kept watch and soothed Vincent through the treatments and the experimentation. It would have made sense for her to be resentful of the workload, yet...

"Really?" She exhaled slowly, softly, as if she, too, was too invested to risk feeling relieved without proper confirmation. Was this born out of genuine concern? Nothing in her demeanour spoke otherwise.

"Really." With no one better to share this moment with, Hosta rushed to hug the woman, barely recalling enough consideration to do it gently so as not to wake the baby in the sling.

"Oh, thank goodness," Ms Underhall mumbled and hugged Hosta back, cheeks wet but smiling.

"No. Thank you. I don't know what I would have done without you!" Having long since succumbed to the thought that she was battling this alone with only an obscure voice helping her in her dreams, Hosta was glad to realise she'd had someone by her side all along. Someone she could see with her own eyes. Someone undoubtedly real who seemed to care. "Please, please go get some sleep. I'll take him for the rest of the night and sleep when you wake up in the morning. We deserve some sleep. This is where the real job starts."

The nanny nodded, loosened the sling and handed the baby over to Hosta carefully enough to not wake him up.

Perhaps, not too long from now, this poor little thing might start sleeping full nights. For the first time, Hosta dared to hope.

"I think it worked!" Hosta said as soon as she realised she was asleep. Likely the voice already knew this, but she couldn't not announce it from her excitement.

It seems to be installing the updates right now. It might take the neural network a while to grow the necessary mycelia to establish the new offshoot because it hasn't done it manually for such a long time. But it should still be able to do it since the renewal processes have been running for centuries without any significant problems.

"How do you know all this?"

My family... I have access to the logs... Never mind. The main thing is it's working. The voice fell silent.

"Are you still there?" Hosta asked.

Yes... Would you like a massage?

Another silence ensued but this time due to Hosta trying to make up her mind.

You can just say no if you don't want one. It's all right.

"No, I..." She really could have used one, but... she was momentarily perplexed over whether it was all right for her to receive one because she was, in fact, married.

As if a mere massage was going to be a problem. But more importantly, as if this sham of a marriage were something she needed to honour even in her dreams.

I know, I'm sorry. I was out of line the last time. Just a massage. Or if you don't want me to touch you, I could run a basic service routine that might help you relax? There wasn't much emotion in this voice, but its speed seemed hasty. A hurried correction of course, then?

"I would like the massage, please," Hosta said and chuckled inwardly. As soon as she could tell the voice was within her reach, she tried her luck.

There was indeed someone there to grab a hold of, someone with a familiar form despite her not being able to see. She pulled them closer and aimed at where she could hear them gasp for breath.

She prayed Vincent was not going to interrupt her now, because the lips she'd found felt soft and comforting against her own, and, after their initial startle, they responded to the kiss.

Oh, oh dear. A massage... The voice became faint. *I meant— Love, just, oh...*

Hosta kissed them again, pleased to have caused such confusion in the normally so matter-of-fact voice.

"It's a massage, *of sorts,*" she reminded them.

Oh, I see. The voice lifted their hand to Hosta's lips. *I sense some stiffness still left...* They returned the kiss with enough force to push Hosta onto her back, and the enthusiasm made her feel giddy and hot all over in a way Walter never had.

Was it because she didn't know who it was? Because it seemed a little naughty considering she was married? Maybe she was into it precisely because she was so disappointed with Walter?

Why do you look like that? What is that expression?

"What?" Worried she'd ruined the mood by worrying too much, Hosta fumbled to find the face the voice belonged to.

It makes me want to— The lips were back, reassuring her that everything was fine.

"By all means," Hosta allowed it. She might have not had a name, a true voice or an image of their face, but she still had the feel of their skin against her fingertips, the warm breaths, taste and shapes she could learn to recognise, and she made damn sure she studied them while there was still night left.

December 1895

"Coffee? Tea?" A woman's voice woke Hosta from her dream.

She was about to respond when she heard a man's voice say, "Whichever you have in that pot. Did it help? If that was her, it was easier than I thought to find her. She looked much younger there, though. She seemed like she was covered in something, so I tried removing it, but I have no idea whether that did anything."

"The numbers look promising, but we won't know until she wakes up. I'm sorry, the coffee is probably cold. I don't have milk or cream, but there's sugar if you prefer." Oh, it was Copper Curls from yesterday, but who was the man? He had his back turned towards Hosta.

"That's all right. I don't enjoy it either way," he said.

"I could have made you some tea," she replied casually. Perhaps he was her husband?

"This is fine." There was something faintly familiar about his voice.

Hosta sat up on the sofa she'd slept on. "Excuse me. Who are you?" she asked.

"Vincent Swifty, nice to meet you." The man turned around and offered her his hand. "I could have sworn we've met, but unfortunately I don't remember where."

Somewhere within her memory, a semblance of this man seemed to exist, if she could only trace her steps far enough through all the holes in that canvas. She stood up to shake his hand.

"The feeling is mutual, it seems, but apparently there's a lot I do not remember."

"Did it get any better since yesterday?" Copper Curls asked.

"Difficult to say. Yesterday is the easiest to recall. Everything else feels like it has happened to someone else a long time ago. This place is no more familiar, and I do not remember either of you two. I suppose this is the Vincent you're hoping to fix?"

If he was her husband, that would explain why she was driven to such lengths. Presumably a happy marriage. How enviable.

"Yes. I have his file here, in case that might refresh your memory." The woman handed Hosta a folder.

"I'm a research assistant, so I don't know what good I will do, but I'll take a look. Oh, is this my handwriting again?"

She'd never seen the folder, but as she looked at it, the pieces seemed to fit together. She was not sixteen. She was not eighteen. And this was him. This was her baby. As some of the memories flooded through her mind, anger was the only thing to stifle the overwhelm.

They had taken her boy once, and she would not let it ever happen again!

She looked up at the woman.

"Where is my baby? What have you done with my baby?" Hosta charged forward, but with the desk between them, the knife she'd pulled fell just short of its target. The man had grabbed a hold of it and her.

"That file is from over three decades ago!" Copper Curls reminded her.

It must have been a few years old... But decades? Hosta backed away. Her hands certainly looked decades older, but whatever remained of her life inside her head didn't seem that much.

Those bastards had taken her baby, hadn't they? She'd been about to retrieve him from the matron that weekend, but when she'd arrived, he had no longer been there. The matron had left to Lingslip. Why had she put him in the workhouse in the first place? Why was that particular memory so hazy? Why would she do that?

Because he was sick?

"I remember having him. I remember he was in my arms. He was crying. I remember he was crying so much, and I couldn't get him to settle..." But then what had happened? She knelt to pick up a photograph that had fallen from the folder. This was him, though, wasn't it? "My baby. Where is he?"

"We don't know. I thought—"

"The restorative index was always so low..." The result of the comparative study had been outright shocking. She'd developed temporary solutions to patch the worst of the issues through a manual connection facilitated by the MOP prototype device, but it had taken numerous tries before any of it had done any good.

She picked up the papers off the floor, reminded of each of her desperate, ghastly efforts to get him to sleep, eat and grow. "I feared he was going to die. He was so sickly. I tried to— I tried everything."

"Do you remember what happened?" Copper Curls knelt next to her.

"I couldn't get him to stop crying. I was alone. He couldn't sleep. I couldn't sleep. I was so tired, I had to do something. The nanny—" She clenched her teeth. "That wretched piece of—" From the corner of her eye, she noticed the man whose face she could now place somewhere within this chaos. Furious beyond reason, she charged at him instead. "You! You vile cockroach, you disgust me!" She grabbed the lapels of his shirt and shoved him against the wall with all her strength.

Too scrawny. A weakling.

"Not you. You are not him." Hosta doubled back. Still seething, she looked elsewhere for her target. "Where is that treacherous, cheating maggot?!"

"There's no one here but us. I'm not sure who you're referring to," Copper Curls said.

"Who else? Walter, my husband, that good-for-nothing whore-monger!" Why were the pieces so slow to slot into place? She could tell there was more still missing, but the bits she'd just recalled were beckoning her to rage.

"I'm sorry. I haven't heard from your husband since the day before yesterday... Vincent?"

Hosta turned her attention to the man cowering where she'd pushed him. They were so similar they had to be related. If she was decades older than she recalled, this must have been one of that dirt bag's crotch-goblins.

"You're his son, aren't you? You're that rat's offspring! I bet you are as disgusting as the treacherous demon that sired you. You look just like him!" She spat, grabbed the coffee cup and saucer from the desk and threw them at him before storming out of the room.

May 1862

Vincent's Restorative Index had taken another dip, and it seemed he was coming down with a chest infection. This was no small matter for such a small child, not to mention someone with such an easily compromised health as Vincent had because of his poor sleep.

Hosta was quick to take every countermeasure as symptoms arose, but the fever did not spare the boy, and he was rendered coughing and bed-bound for several days.

It was at times like this, Hosta found herself wishing Walter hadn't been such an insufferable oaf, because another child might have meant she could have kept making progress on the research even while Vincent was recuperating. Now, she was forced to turn her attention to other things until the boy was in better health to withstand the tests and the treatments.

Because the situation remained precarious, Hosta stayed in the nursery most of the day. To make the best use of her time, she tended to some paperwork for an unrelated sponsored research study she had taken on to earn a bit of money for the boy's treatments.

At least the MOP device seemed to be working flawlessly now, although it still needed some finetuning before she dared to use it to tamper with Vincent's memory. So far she'd only tried it on herself to remove single minutes at a time. The voice had been able to send Vincent some 'patches' through the 'link' but nothing that had made a significant difference to Vincent's connection when he wasn't connected to the device.

The nanny had yet again stayed up the previous night to help Hosta, and she'd done it so many times that, by now, the dark circles around her eyes seemed permanent. It was a surprise that the woman hadn't quit or ever even mentioned quitting, considering how hard she worked.

"You can go," Hosta told her. It was best to let the nanny rest because she would likely have to stay up tonight also.

"Thank you." She frowned but did not turn down the offer.

"Know what?" Vincent said and sat up shakily in his bed.

"Nothing, dear. Go back to sleep." The nanny tucked him back in.

"Walter?" The boy sounded delirious. "Oh, you mean Papa? You're going to Papa?"

Hosta reached for the thermometer thinking it might be time to check his fever again.

"Shhh, sleep, dear." The hint of worry in the nanny's voice prompted Hosta to pay more attention to their conversation.

"Don't go, Ma." The boy reached up to take the nanny by the sleeve. The nanny glanced at Hosta, and the look on her face confirmed she'd understood the implications of Vincent's words.

It could have been the fever, but in all honesty, Hosta had expected this moment to come eventually. The woman did take better care of Vincent than Hosta ever could. She stifled the nagging irritation and waved for the woman to leave.

"No! Don't go!" Vincent repeated.

"It's all right. Your Mama is there. She'll stay with you."

"But I don't like Papa when he does those things to you. Don't go. You can't leave."

The nanny's face grew pale. It took Hosta a moment to connect the dots.

"What does Walter do?" Hosta asked the nanny, but when the woman took a step back and pursed her lips, the boy seemed more forthcoming, so she asked him instead. "What does your Papa do to your Mama?"

The boy looked confused and turned to the nanny.

"Why not? Why can't I tell her? I don't want Papa to do that anymore."

"What does Walter do?" Hosta asked again from anyone willing to answer.

The nanny looked too guilty to be hiding bruises, but Hosta grabbed her by the wrist and lifted her sleeves to check just in case. "If he doesn't beat you, what does he do?"

"No! No hurt Mama!" Vincent sat up again. "No, no, no, no, no! I don't want! No hurt Mama!"

"Does he beat you?!" Hosta tightened her hold on the nanny's wrist.

"No!" The nanny looked away. "He doesn't, but it's not what you think. The boy is young. He has a fever. He must have misunderstood."

"I don't believe you." At this point in the marriage, it was easy to imagine Walter doing whatever the hell he pleased, but even if theirs wasn't a real friendship, having the nanny betray her hurt worse. If she'd been after Hosta's husband all the while, with such a straight face, there was no trusting her.

The familiar explosive anger brewed within Hosta as she clenched her jaw to not explode. The bulk of her anger was firmly directed at Walter for tainting and ruining the only trustworthy person she'd had left in her life. Why couldn't he have kept his filthy claws off of the woman?

Hosta was done putting up with this sham of a marriage, and carried by her fiery resolve, she did not hesitate to seek her target.

December 1895

Mind fixed to leaving this wretched place, Hosta was doubly irked to be interrupted before she could exit the building, even when the primary object of her wrath had so conveniently marched right in her path.

"I gave you until Midwinter to cure my daughter. Where is she?" A pathetic, shrivelled version of Walter grabbed her by the arm.

"I know nothing of any filthy crotchlings you may have begotten!" Hosta snarled at him purely out of instinct. "Did you make some with her? Were they as faulty as the one you forced upon me?" She glared at the woman standing a few steps behind him. She didn't seem to have aged half as much as everyone else. That hardly seemed fair.

Hosta looked away and noticed the bearded Walter lookalike standing at the bottom of the stairs. She hadn't the time to concern herself with the man, though, because Walter tightened his grip on her arm and opened his putrid gob again.

"You will not speak another word about my daughter, or I will rip that depraved tongue right out of your mouth!"

Daughter. Daughter. What daughter? She could tell there was still something stored somewhere inside her head—an improvement to the day before—but she couldn't quite access the details.

"I have held my end of our agreement," Walter continued his raving. "I've honoured your husband's outrageous demands and stayed out of your way all these years when you've been messing around, trying to fix your half-witted progeny. I've even given you a more than courteous chance to study my daughter, so long as you make sure she has no memory of it when you return her to me. I will not repeat this again. Where is she? Where did you stash my daughter?"

"Get it through to your thick skull, Walter, I would never have any interest in something that's originated from your shrivelled, scabby ball sac!" Whoever it was, she was no concern of hers. None of this made much sense. Didn't the man have another son, not a daughter…?

Walter was still at it with the insults. Once done with them, he lowered his tone and said, "I should have known the two of you weren't to be trusted. She is not here, is she? I swear to the Guardian you're going to pay for this." He had the gall to shake his fist at her. What an insufferable nincompoop!

"It's true I have no vapid wench here to gift you, but you can take your defective excuse of a son if you please!" she told him.

"I have no son!" Walter roared in one of his fits of rage and grabbed both of Hosta's arms as if that would make it more threatening. True, he could have crushed her without a second thought, but no matter what the danger, there was no way she would give this man the satisfaction of seeing her take him seriously. Walter was a joke, and as such, only worth a hearty cackle.

When Hosta shook her hand loose to point at the lookalike at the bottom of the stairs, Walter pushed her aside, and the violent shove forced her to her knees. The memories were definitely still there, but as long as she kept laughing, it seemed like they would stay comfortably at an arm's length.

Hosta's laugh was cut off by an ominous whack and the sound of something heavy hitting the stairs with several consecutive thumps. She looked up to where Walter had stood, momentarily confused to see the woman who had previously cowered behind Walter there instead, holding the ceremonial torch of the Guardian with such a fierce expression on her face.

"But I do. I have a son. You bastard," the woman said.

The other end of the torch fell with a heavy thunk, spilling the rest of the embers in its cup onto the floor. That was for sure about to light this glorified wooden hut on fire within a matter of minutes and likely thus take care of the evidence. However, running out the front door without so much as trying to put out the fire would look suspicious. All in all, this did not seem like a situation one wanted to associate oneself with.

"As for you, I did you a favour. Then and now," the surprisingly feisty nanny interrupted Hosta's thoughts.

"I'm about to return that favour. We need to leave!" Hosta attempted to herd her down the stairs, but she resisted.

"Why down? The door—"

"Do you want to be blamed for this?"

"No."

"Then you'd better not run out the front door in broad daylight!" Hosta pulled her along by force, and thankfully she stopped resisting. At the bottom of the stairs, Hosta turned to Copper Curls, "You know this place. Where was that door we used yesterday?"

"This way."

The door in the break room was jammed by snow. The Walter lookalike pushed at it, but one couldn't exactly call him muscular or dependable, and he only managed to crack it open enough to fit a hand through.

"It's no use. Why the hell do they always have to open outwards?" The man pulled his scuffed up and chill-reddened hand back inside.

"Fire safety." Copper Curls checked the corridor. "It sounds like the fire might be spreading down here. There's smoke."

"Are there any other doors?"

"Probably, but I don't know the place well enough to know where."

"Anything to break the door with? An axe?"

"No. But there's a skylight in my office next door."

Having heard their conversation, Hosta hurried back into the corridor that had already started to fill with smoke. She crouched down and signalled to the nanny to do the same in case she was too daft to realise the air was more breathable lower down.

Hosta could hear Walter's offspring coughing behind her, and something about this made her want to tell him off for being too stupid to crouch, but then, a glance in his direction was enough to tell her he must have been doing his best to do just that. There seemed to be something the matter with his knee.

Thank the Guardian, the office was still clear from smoke!

"Move aside and face away." The man grabbed the desk lamp and used it to crack the skylight. It took him a good deal of whacking before the skylight collapsed, bringing with it a hefty load of snow, most of which landed on him as he was too silly to take his own advice and step aside. The current of air drew in a thick cloud of smoke from the corridor, and it soon filled the office, worsening his cough.

"Let's move the desk," Copper Curls suggested. Good thing she had some meat on her bones as that desk would not have moved with Vincent's strength alone. Why was he so skinny...?

"Watch out for the glass," the man said, helped the nanny up onto the desk and gave Hosta an unneeded push when she climbed up on her own. Admittedly, the distance from the desk and up through the skylight was too much for this old body to handle, so Hosta was grateful for the next leg up. But she was hardly a cripple and could mostly take care of herself.

The nanny helped her pull Vera up next, but with no one pushing from below, Hosta could already tell they would not be able to pull Vincent up the same way.

"Give me your hand!" Vera still seemed adamant to try, so Hosta looked around for anything that might have been useful: a piece of rope, a plank... but everything was covered by the snow.

"Vincent! Give me your hand!" Vera was stretching out her hand to him and grabbed him by the forearm. "Up! Now!" She seemed to struggle with the grip, and Hosta was much too far to help even when she'd inched as close as she could.

The wind distorted half of what they were saying, but it looked as though Vincent was starting to panic. The man disappeared from view as more smoke billowed into the office, through the skylight and into their faces.

Chapter 8

May 1862

Hosta breathed in rapid succession, mind drawn to that simple action as if she couldn't trust her body to do an adequate job of it. Somewhere beyond the loud hum in her ears, the door was slammed shut, and she was left alone in the room: her father's study with mostly the same furniture but with Walter's things scattered in it, now across the floor in an unfamiliar chaos.

She needed these things out of her sight, so, with not much mind left to think about it, she yanked open a window and started tossing them out.

Out. All of it. She'd lost touch with her anger, but her drive to be rid of it all remained. Anything that wasn't supposed to be in here she threw out the window as quickly as her body could shift it: item after item crashing on the street below, leaving her hands before she even knew what she was carrying. Out. Out.

A sickening, sinking feeling gripped her the second she let go of the birdcage, but it was already flying through the air. Hosta gasped, her brain catching up with what she'd just done, and she reached out the window to see the cage hit the cobbles below with a crash—with the bird flapping frantically inside.

She watched it in shock, still flapping in the cage. Her breathing would not settle no matter how she tried to control it. That was Vincent's bird. That was not— that was—

Was it hurt? She looked back inside, urged to run down the stairs to see whether she had hurt the bird, but Walter was still in the house. She felt light-headed and could not bring herself to calm down.

Am I insane? Have I lost it? She looked back out the window where the bird's flapping had mostly ceased. *Was it dead? Did I kill it?*

Her mind emptied itself from all coherent thought, and she stared down with her mouth still open.

"Are you all right, missus?" A man from below shouted up at her.

She knew she was supposed to say something back, but no words came to mind that could have reached her lips. All she could do was stare at him with her mouth open until she regained at least some control over herself and managed to close her mouth and withdraw from the window. Even after she'd done that, she stared at her hands unable to do much else.

Speak. Speak. Speak.

The only thing out of her mouth were the increasingly rough breaths she was taking. Her hands were trembling. Her eyes felt dry, stinging and smarting.

She sat down on the floor to rock herself. Hurts. Hurts. Make it stop. Make it—

I killed the bird.

Calm down. It may not have died. It was dead. The marriage was dead. Her father was dead. Vincent—

She stood up in an instant and ran out of the study and into the nursery. The nanny was still in there, but one look at Hosta and the woman retreated from the room.

Vincent. Alive. Still alive. The boy looked so frail the way he was. Too frail. Hosta didn't dare to touch him.

Need to fix. Can't get attached. Can't feel for this sorry little thing that might die at any moment. Can't—

She closed her eyes and hung on to the end of the boy's bed. Fix it so it's safe. Fix him so he doesn't break. Fix him so he can handle me. Make him stronger so he doesn't die on me.

She opened her eyes and looked around the room. The MOP device, her notes, the progress. She needed more funding because she couldn't rely on Walter anymore. Not that she'd relied on him much before, but the medicine and the upkeep were all so very expensive. This was a priority.

The nanny. She needed a new nanny. It was all so expensive. She needed a plan. And for the next five hours until she passed out from exhaustion, she directed her mind to fixing the problem.

The darkness remained as dark as always, but now it was also silent. Hosta waited for any soothing words that could have made her feel better, but there were none.

The way she was still struggling to put her thoughts into words while awake, perhaps it really had been something within her, an inner voice, that she'd broken with her rage? And if it were just her imagination supplying her with a distraction to keep her sane amidst all this, perhaps it might return once she'd regained her composure?

Walter left with the nanny the following morning. Finding a new nanny at such a short notice was impossible, so Hosta rang her mother and arranged for her to take Vincent for the time being until she could get this mess sorted out.

With no man in the house, it took Hosta several frustrating days to rearrange the business-related services and deliveries previously done by Walter. It was time away from research and finding a cure for Vincent.

Four days later, Hosta's mother rang saying she would be leaving to see family in Chattsmouth and couldn't take a gravely ill child there along with her. Vincent was moved to Hosta's cousin's house until Hosta could pick him up. Only, she was too busy with desperately trying to get the suppliers to acknowledge her in Walter's stead, so with the business and her income at stake, she could not afford to take any time off to take care of the boy.

That was when the mild-mannered young man from next door, James Craft, swooped in to help her with the practicalities.

The Crafts were long-time acquaintances of Hosta's mother, so it wasn't as if Hosta was letting a complete stranger into her life. James had always been polite and kind, so Hosta had no real objections to his advances when he started courting her. After all, any divorced woman with a child could count her blessings if a man showed any interest in her, no matter if she was in possession of her own house and business—which Hosta had managed to secure for herself by threatening Walter with nefarious curses should he try to make her existence any more difficult.

James's family was already wealthy enough for him to not be eyeing Hosta for her meagre possessions, so she felt confident enough that she wasn't about to be taken advantage of. Even better, once the man proposed to her, this reopened her chances of producing another child that might help solve what was wrong with Vincent.

James was also very knowledgeable about engineering and chemistry and had a knack for understanding the 'documentation' and the MOP device. With his help, Hosta was able to refine it enough to feel more comfortable using it on Vincent to smooth out some of his recent, more unpleasant memories.

Vincent's health hadn't improved much, and it wasn't long before Hosta's cousin saddled another more distant member of the family to take care of him. When Hosta hadn't heard from her cousin after a week, she rang after and heard they had passed Vincent on to someone who had taken him to the workhouse in Dritsby.

All the while, everyone Hosta rang or asked for information seemed strangely unwilling to share the details of how Vincent was doing and why they had passed him on, always reciting one shady-sounding excuse or another.

The matron of the workhouse seemed like a reasonable lady, and it was a relief to finally speak to someone willing to give Hosta an actual update on the boy. A little rattled by the process of tracking Vincent down, Hosta was glad that he seemed to be somewhere stable and secure for now.

Perhaps he was better off there while she got things in order for him? Certainly, with the situation with James moving forward, the upcoming wedding and the possibility of a baby in the near future, it would be nicer to bring Vincent home when things had settled down.

CHAPTER 9

June 1879

H osta had never been fond of the Chest, particularly where it extended beyond the Realm of the Crown. But now that she'd finally caught up with the damn boy near Stoatness, she wasn't about to let her distaste of the local culture and its loud manners get in the way of the latest round of treatments.

Vincent's behaviour the past couple of years had seemed erratic, although it was difficult to tell whether this was due to his condition or the normal curiosity of a boy on an adventure on his own for the first time. He was still much less of a cause for worry than his wayward younger brother, who'd completely disappeared from the face of the earth for the second summer in a row.

Regardless of the circumstances, Hosta was glad Vincent had finally taken a breather from all the running around because her body was about to burst in the third trimester of her fifth pregnancy, even if it wasn't as cumbersome as the twins' and even if she was still feeling much more energetic than during the first trimester.

"What's this?" Hosta was given a piece of paper by the servant of the house she was visiting while in Stoatness.

"It's from the same gentleman who came by two days ago, madam." The boy bowed and waited to be excused. Hosta waved him away to read the latest report in private.

Apparently, Vincent was currently still spending time with the Vesper girl, but this time in seemingly less indulgent settings than with any of the girls before: they had been seen at a nearby park merely chatting and eating sandwiches. How unimaginative.

"But I suppose it's better than what I need to deal with at home," she reminded herself.

Even after deploying the same search network she regularly used to track down Vincent, she'd had one measly sighting of Julian in early April near Lingslip and could only hope this year followed the same pattern as the last, and the blistering butthole found his way back home come autumn, preferably before the baby was born. He'd been a right mess when he'd returned the year before, but at least he'd been alive.

Jonathan was safe at home with James and the nanny, but James would soon voice his displeasure if Hosta kept prioritising her first-born over his children, especially in her condition. Enduring the trip home would only get more uncomfortable from this point on. She didn't have much time to waste.

Hosta's host had gracefully granted her a small study to use for whenever she came by, which was usually about once a year for a local herbalists' gathering. Since the study was only in infrequent guest use the rest of the year, she'd made use of the space to house her travel treatment kit and a locked cabinet of reports and research notes she'd collected in the past few years since trailing Vincent and monitoring his progress.

She pulled out the slim file she had for the Vesper family and flicked through it to refresh her memory. They were an unremarkable bunch, and the girl seemed nothing special, so likely Vincent would soon tire of her and move on. That meant Hosta needed to be quick about intercepting him to give him his treatment while it was still even remotely convenient.

"Excuse me, madam." The servant was back with another note. Hosta glared at him for interrupting, took the note and shooed him away.

"Park Road, 16:00." A date? At a library? Where was the excitement in that? Hosta shook her head exasperated. Presumably Vincent would be easiest to get a hold of after meeting with the girl, though, and with the treatment taken care of, he'd be free to explore and waste his youth for another few months until the effects wore off again. That would hopefully mean one less thing for her to worry about so she could concentrate on finding Julian... Although the baby probably should have been her number one priority right now? She patted her belly and sighed.

This was her ticket to roam for now. She'd let James have his way the first time, thinking he'd wanted another baby because of what had happened to Justin, but this seemed more and more like a jealous attempt at chaining her down to keep her from pursuing Vincent's treatment. It was curious how James was more willing to let her go when she was carrying another child for him and thus guaranteed to return—as if she'd chase Vincent endlessly if that weren't the case, and as if she had somewhere better to go.

She just needed to take care of this and get back to her research. She only hoped the years had wisened her enough to not repeat the same mistakes, that she'd be able to save Julian somehow and that

Jonathan and the baby had a brighter future ahead of them than their three older siblings.

"Excuse me, madam," the damned servant interrupted her for the third time and handed her another note.

Hosta glanced at it and rolled her eyes. The speeder had been sighted leaving the city in a hurry. Already? What about the library date?

Damn the boy! Why was he so fickle and hopeless?! Hosta felt a morsel of compassion for the poor girl so easily discarded like worn-out rags but more so for herself for having to continue this wretched chase.

Nevertheless, she decided the least she could do was to send the girl to a decent school in Gobehurst or Chattsmouth on some made up scholarship or another as compensation for having had to deal with her inconsiderate, immature dolt of a son. Perhaps she would make something of herself instead of wasting her time on such no good relationships.

December 1895

Since the Vesper girl seemed so unwilling to give up, Hosta bit her teeth and tried to grab a hold of whatever she could to help. Together, they would manage to hold Vincent in the air for a few seconds, but it wasn't nearly enough for him to hoist himself up the rest of the way.

It was the most awful feeling to look down there and see Walter's wretched face look back at her, yet that same face made her insides clench with fear like Walter's never had.

"It's no good. We're wasting time." She let go.

"You can't say that! What kind of a mother are you?!" Aurora screamed at her.

"A bad one! But I'm not stupid." Shouting back at the woman didn't change the fact that Hosta had wasted precious minutes trying to grab a hold of Vincent when the correct solution was embarrassingly obvious had she only bothered to think about it rationally. "Drop him down before he suffocates!"

The nanny turned to look at her, hesitated briefly, but let go. For a moment, Hosta was baffled by this show of trust when the Vesper girl still held on so stubbornly.

But there was no time to wonder or argue about it. Hosta ran to the recessed entrance and clawed at the snow until her fingers felt like brittle, icy sticks, and her lungs wheezed and burned. The nanny was soon clawing next to her with equal fervour, and thankfully so, because even with Aurora joining in a moment later, it still took them ages to get the door to open, and by the end of it, all Hosta could do was curse her useless, feeble body for failing her.

"Who knows what's in the smoke in there, so crouch as low down as you can, and try not to breathe it in," Aurora said. Hosta let her take the lead, gladly, as she could barely hold herself upright, and somebody needed to save her stupid boy.

The smoke stung in her eyes, but she dove in behind Aurora and willed her limbs to move while they still needed to move.

Vincent was on the ground in the office, thankfully still conscious and crawling towards them when they entered. Aurora pulled him up to his feet, but she was not quite strong enough to carry him on her own, so, already tired to the bone and mostly useless herself, Hosta was eternally grateful for having the nanny also aiding the rescue.

Lillian... no, Lilya? Her name still loomed there in the shrouded recesses.

The foundations of the building creaked and moaned around them. Tufts of thick, black smoke and heat rushed into the break room. The air was heavy with the putrid stench of chemicals.

"You! Ram it! More! Open it wider," Hosta ordered Lilya so she could force Vincent through the door and into the fresh, cold air. Aurora pulled him under his armpits and up the stairs with Hosta dragging him by his clothes from the side.

The air outside was fresh, but it was freezing and harsh to breathe in, so as soon as Vincent was out of danger, Hosta collapsed into a heap to cough and to gasp for air. Her body trembled violently, gripped by the cold, but also by the shock that she'd almost lost him again without realising.

What if she hadn't remembered...? Her eyes hurt. Her throat hurt. Everything hurt so much she couldn't breathe. If she'd remembered even a few minutes later, she might have not made the effort. It might have been too late.

She felt frail in the face of the fear squeezing her heart, but something warm enveloped her, easing it slowly. A cloak? Hosta looked up.

"Lilya?"

"It's all right. I'm here. That was scary, wasn't it?"

Yes. Yes it was. But it was fine, now, right? Hosta turned to see where her son lay in the snow with Aurora cradling his head.

"Are you cold?" the woman asked Vincent.

"I've been colder. This is nothing." He was responding to her, at least.

"Is he delirious?" Hosta asked. She needed to pull herself together. This cloak, though kind, was wasted on her, so she crawled to Vincent and draped it over him instead. "Has someone called the firemen?"

"Yes," Lilya responded, apparently having already walked some ways further afield to check. "I saw at least two fire engines arrive. There were men pumping water and locals moving more snow to keep it contained. It looks like it's all going to burn, but it might not take anything else along with it."

"All of that research, all of the precious texts, gone in an instant." Aurora's voice was barely audible. Vincent raised his hand to her cheek, and she looked back at him. "It's heartbreaking, but it's not the end of the world. Let's get you somewhere inside."

Indeed. Hosta shuddered. What good was any of it if he had suffocated to death in there? How deep was the trench of her incompetence for almost letting that happen? She squeezed her fists and schooled these questions out of her mind.

"All right." Vincent pushed himself up to sit, but it didn't look like he would be doing much walking based on his grimace.

The nearest shelter was across the yard at... her house. But it didn't seem a wise choice right now. Lilya was also looking at the back door as if suggesting it.

"I'd advise against going in there," Hosta said. "It was not a pretty sight yesterday, and I can't imagine a day has done it any good. Besides, not exactly where you want to be if you want to stay out of trouble with the law..." She realised her son was now looking straight at her.

How long had it been since? When—? Her heart started fumbling its beats, making her dizzy until she coughed to force it back to a steady rhythm.

"Thank you for pulling me out," Vincent said but quickly turned back to Aurora. "Ren is probably waiting with the cat. Right?"

"Yes. We should head over there, but first..." Aurora scooped some snow to wipe the blood off his face. She treated him so tenderly and with such affection, perhaps it was safe to entrust her with him? "It looks like I have nowhere to be this Midwinter's Eve, so if the offer is still valid..."

Would that make him happy? Or would he still try to make a run for it regardless of the knee injury?

"Of course it is!" he responded. He certainly looked like he might be ready this time.

CHAPTER 10

December 1895

"And you, missus?" The little girl asked Hosta.

Hosta looked up at the slightly dishevelled yet handsome grown man who had so selflessly helped them out of a burning building with little regard for his own safety, who was holding himself together while attentive to the needs of the people around him—even those of a small child that wasn't really his.

She'd seen this man many times before but mostly as a source of worry and from a distance. This was one of fewer than a handful of times he had ever looked back at her since early childhood, though, and she wasn't about to miss her opportunity.

"My name is Hosta Aelia." Her eyes burned, but she did not dare to look away from Vincent's gaze. "I believe I gave birth to a boy, whom I loved dearly, but who was too much for my young selfish self to handle. He got caught in the middle of my war with the world and had to pay a price that wasn't his to pay. It doesn't weigh much in the scheme of things, but should it bring you any consolation, I am truly sorry. I don't remember what I've done all these years or whether it was something irredeemable. I certainly do not expect to be forgiven. But I want you to know that from where I'm standing and what I know right now, I feel like I would have done everything in my power to help you."

"Everything?" He looked surprised. Well, he would be...

"Yes. Seeing as you are still struggling, I must have failed. Tell me, are you unhappy with your life? It may be too late for me to get caught up with the research to start again, and you don't have to have anything to do with me if you so wish, but would you want me to do that? Try to fix it while I have life in me, I mean."

"Why did you give me up if you meant to do everything to help me?"

The answer to that question stung at the back of Hosta's throat. She could recall the circumstances that had led to that situation. She knew the logistics. Even as she recited them to her son, she wished she could have shaken herself awake, to stop herself from making such a colossal mistake. But the convenience of it had dangled in front of her like a freshly steaming slice of apple pie. "I wish I could have kept you close to me, but at least I knew where you were at all times. Until... until..." Most of her memories were hazy, but she could just about tug at their corners to shake the dust off. This one, however, seemed like a casket nailed shut. "I can't remember. I think they must have placed you without my knowledge. The matron was always so suspicious when I came to give you your treatments and take the latest data. I told her you wouldn't remember any of it no matter how unpleasant those experimental treatments may have seemed, but she must have not believed me. I don't remember much beyond that, but I would assume I did everything in my power to get them to return you to me. If that didn't happen, I'm so sorry, I must have failed you."

Perhaps if she'd seemed more human in the matron's eyes, the woman wouldn't have kept him from her? But this was just another failure in a long list of failures.

"To answer your question, no, I'm not unhappy," Vincent said. "I can't say it has always been a pleasure, but right now I'm ready to go spend Midwinter's Eve with my brother and our loved ones—" He turned to Aurora abruptly and started wiggling his fingers at Hosta, excited. "Didn't you say she was Julian's—?"

Aurora seemed to understand what he was getting at and opened her mouth in similar surprise.

"How many—? Do they all start with J? Now I feel left out!" He seemed about to sulk.

"What are you talking about?" Hosta remained confused.

"Ah, come inside and close the door. I guess there are a few more things we need to talk about as we get ourselves cleaned up," Vincent said, and thus, apparently, the conversation had moved on to other things without sufficient explanations.

What 'all start with J'? Julian? The name was familiar, but it also made Hosta feel distinctly uncomfortable, as if something invisible was wrenching her insides.

"That might be more practical, considering we only have these two rooms, and there's not much space in the washroom," Vincent was saying. "Ren, could you be a dear and fetch a towel just for me, then?"

Julian? Hosta lifted her finger still hoping to ask. This seemed important, but they were so busy fussing over something else...

"What time is it? Almost noon? How about we come back here at three o'clock and head to Rhys's together?" Aurora suggested.

"We...?" Was she included in this? Had they invited her?

"Unless you have somewhere else to be? If there's someone after you, you'd probably be safest with us for now until you figure out what you want to do. Unless that had something to do with Mr Wakefield?"

"No, I don't know who those people were." Even if the men at the house had had something to do with Walter, they were still out there. It wouldn't hurt to be among people she considered at least moderately safe until she could clear up this mess inside her head. "If it's not too imposing, I will take you up on your offer."

"Then it's settled."

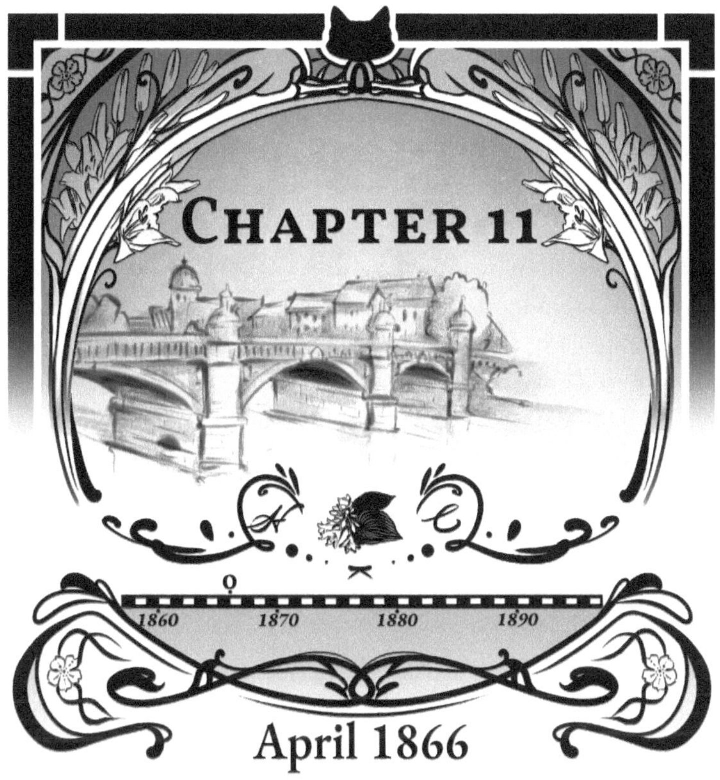

CHAPTER 11

April 1866

The issues had become more noticeable by the time the twins turned three. Justin had always been more quiet than Julian, and while the two were identical in looks, they were usually easy to tell apart by temperament. Julian began to voice discontent over the various testing Hosta had incorporated into the twins' daily routines as well as the lack of attention they received as she was busy with something they could not understand.

Initially, Hosta attributed the symptoms to the environment or the twins not receiving enough nurture despite the elderly nanny she'd hired to look after them. Before long it became clear Julian was abnormally prone to temper tantrums despite any interventions or support he was given. He was much less able to control his outbursts than his brother, even though the two were developing at an otherwise similar pace.

On an evening of a particularly stressful day when the twins had momentarily been left unsupervised in their playroom after dinner, things took a dreadful turn.

It only took a moment for Justin to swallow something he really wasn't supposed to: a substance Julian had pilfered from the exam room that morning presumably because it was in a pretty bright green bottle or because he had been peeved about being forced to do the tests every day.

He was only three years old. There was no way for him to understand what was in it. Similarly, Justin only understood the novelty of a new toy gifted to him by his trusty brother. He was no longer at an age to wantonly chew on everything he could get his grabby hands on, but he was curious, and his teeth were a convenient tool to pry loose the stopper.

If one were to look for the person to blame, perhaps it was Hosta herself, passed out in the next room, exhausted by having spent most nights of the previous half a year searching for any trace of her firstborn son when she should have shown more interest in her immediate family. Perhaps it was James who was downstairs prioritising securing the funding for her latest research. Perhaps it was the nanny who had stepped out of the room to fetch a fresh shirt for the boy who had spilled food all over his during dinner—incidentally, the same boy about to ingest a substantial amount of calomel aka mercurous chloride.

The severity of the situation did not become apparent until much later when Justin began to show signs of acute mercury poisoning, and by then, it was much too late to do anything about it.

May 1876

Hosta breathed in the darkness. Between Justin's newest bout of seizures and reports from Julian's school, she'd not had a decent night's sleep for weeks since the move to Firth, so it did not come as a surprise that she'd fallen asleep when she'd really only meant to stretch herself and rest on the bed for a moment.

Justin was in no condition to go to school, but Julian still needed to, so the most logical solution was to have him board at least until Justin was well enough to attend. She just needed to get the seizures to stop.

Julian had not taken it well, but his worsening moods and aggression had been taking a toll on Justin, so separating them was necessary.

None of this would have happened if the damn boys hadn't played with what they weren't supposed to all those years ago. It had been a stressful decade of dealing with the aftermath of the poisoning and Justin's developmental delays and weakened constitution, but the mess would have never become this bad if it weren't for Julian always causing trouble!

The latest incident had really put Hosta on edge, and she was glad that Julian was now out of her hair and someone else's issue for the time being. The Guardian-cursed thief had been pinching laudanum from the storage room for months before getting caught, and the state he'd been in when he'd been cut off that stuff had made these some of the toughest weeks Hosta had had to manage since the twins had been born.

The withdrawal was what had caused the latest series of Justin's seizures, and they were still ongoing even once the worst had passed for Julian. The damn boy could have served to suffer for a while longer for the way these seizures had put Justin's usual treatments on hold and placed his life in danger.

At least Vincent's latest course of treatments last year seemed to have worked well because it looked like his condition was now stable. But all this meant that Hosta had to spend all of her waking hours trying to keep Justin from getting any worse, and she was bone-tired of the long nights in the lab as well as her usual efforts to secure more funding to pay for these treatments.

At least the darkness was not going to berate her for her selfish thoughts or remind her of her own poor choices or the regret that she hadn't been more careful with the storage room keys or keeping an eye on her boys. No one here was going to shoulder her with the guilt of hiring a second nanny when she should have devoted her time and existence to her boys. No one would absolve her from that guilt either.

There was no sense in delving in self-pity or self-loathing when she needed to rest so she could face her hell again when she woke up.

So why was she spending any of her precious energy on crying?

Oh, dear! Are you all right?

The touch of a hand brushing Hosta's cheek yanked her from her thoughts. She fell back in an instant as if there were something in this darkness to fall back to. But she hadn't heard the voice for years, and hearing it again brought back a raging force of pent up feelings.

"Why did you leave?! You said you'd stay if I needed you!"

For a good few years, she'd wondered if the voice had really just been a manifestation of her inner self comforting her when she'd most needed it, and that it had disappeared because she'd developed this strange, crooked, self-enamoured relationship with it when she'd sensed her marriage was about to end.

No one could have cared about her the way she cared about herself, so surely that must have been a figment of her imagination? The only thing that theory did not explain was the voice's involvement in providing the information and the credentials for the MOP to work, but that could have been the Guardian itself trying to provide assistance.

Oh, love. Please don't cry. Don't cry... Someone enveloped Hosta in their arms and stroked her back to comfort her. On the off chance this wasn't just her imagination or the Guardian somehow humouring her with an illusion, if it was indeed a real person, then they must have been able to see her in the darkness. How else would they know she was crying, bawling her eyes out like this, unable to stop the tears even when she could stifle the sounds? How embarrassing for anyone to see her like this.

What happened? Can you tell me?

"Why did you leave?!" Hosta tried to take a swipe at whoever it was in front of her. Her hand hit something soft and tangible. If this really was just a dream supplied by the Guardian, it felt disconcertingly real. She could have sworn there was someone with a form right in front of her despite her not seeing a thing. She could almost remember its shape if she strained her memory enough.

Ouch... A sound of shuffling as the person presumably retreated from her range. *I'm sorry. I didn't realise you still needed me. Please don't be angry.*

"You promised me!" Hosta fed her anger to stifle the tears. "I could have used someone when Walter left me to deal with Vincent alone! When Vincent got so sick I feared he would die! When my aunt's sister in law placed him in a bloody workhouse because she couldn't deal with him! When the cursed matron sent him off to who knows where without my knowledge and hid him from me!" She drew a sharp breath. "Where the hell were you when I had to search the continent for my boy?! Where were you when Julian started presenting with anger issues? When he stole a bottle of calomel and gave it to his brother? During the countless weeks I fought to save my boys? When I ran out of funding and had to sell my soul for it? When Julian started self-medicating with laudanum, and Justin was overcome with seizures?" She ran out of steam and breath as the last of it squeezed out of her like bile after vomit.

I'm so sorry. I never realised...

Who was the voice to know so many things as if reading her mind but not see these things as they unfolded? Was it really not herself or the Guardian? It would have been less painful had it been a dream all along.

"Where were you?" There wasn't enough anger to drown how she felt. Hosta slumped to the floor. Someone hovered over her and stroked her hair.

I'm sorry. I would have come sooner had I known. How is Vincent? How are the twins? Where are they? Should I run the diagnostics routine?

"I sent Julian to a boarding school once he was off the laudanum. Justin is in the second recovery room at the clinic recovering from the seizure today, but he's stable. I'm thinking I need to somehow detach the twins from one another so that Julian doesn't keep making it worse. My theory is that the Guardian struggles to identify them, so even when I'm careful with targeting the treatments, some trickle through to Julian. Same if I try to do anything with Julian..." Explaining it to someone took Hosta's mind momentarily off the disturbing recurring mental image of Justin convulsing amidst a seizure. "I've developed a device that does the diagnostic routine for me via an improved version of the MOP, but the output is often too garbled for me to understand."

James had been building various prototypes according to Hosta's specifications utilising the MOP's credentials, but there were too many pieces still missing of the so-called 'documentation' and no sign of the fabled 'user manual' no matter how far and wide Hosta searched.

I'll run it for you immediately. I just need to locate Justin's signature. How is Vincent? Is he all right?

"Vincent is fine, for the time being. He's riding around with that speeder of his acting like a right fool, but he's old enough to do whatever the hell he pleases..." He'd been drinking and courting girls for a time but seemed to have grown tired of it fairly quickly in favour of travelling and getting into other kinds of trouble. "The connection is no better than before, but I got the Guardian to force the ReST according to a set schedule if he doesn't get enough otherwise, so he's been stable for a few years now. Sometimes I track him down to make sure everything is still running smoothly, but so far it's been doing its job."

I think I've located Justin. Ah, I see. Yes, the Guardian thinks it's a single signature split up into two. The access markers aren't identical, but they are both similarly corrupted, so the system can't tell them apart.

"Is there a way to fix it?"

I will look into it, but unfortunately I don't know much about the access markers themselves, how they're formed or where they are stored. The best chance would be to fix the GateKeeper module, but I don't have the credentials to make any alterations to the system. Maybe if you could find someone who had the right credentials?

"Most people I've talked to about the Guardian think it's a deity and that the documentation is some holy scripture open to interpretation. I've never heard anyone mention 'credentials' before you, so I imagine it might take precious time I don't have to find someone."

I can try to apply one of the patches in the old libraries, but that's a shot in the dark.

"How risky is it? I can't afford to..." No matter how much of a nuisance these boys were for her, she'd invested too much to bear the thought of losing either of them. "I can't take any risks, but I need to fix it somehow."

I'll do everything I can to help you.

Lillian Wakefield helped her seven-year-old daughter down from the train car. It had been a long and unpleasant ride from Dritsby to Firth not only because of the unsteadiness of the train but also because of little Iris's insistence she wasn't going to be wearing her hair tied up or her new shoes or hat.

Iris was currently shoeless and sulking on the platform looking like she might want to tear off her dress in the next moment, so Lillian tried to distract her by handing her her little travel bag to carry.

"Let's go, dear." Lillian took Iris's hand and pulled her along before she could cause a scene. Her socks would be ruined, but they were not worth the hassle of fighting over the shoes, and the girl was too heavy to carry all the way from the station to the clinic. "Watch your step."

T he building at the address she'd been given looked about as modest as the doctor's office in Grovestead where the Wakefield family would normally visit, and, against the backdrop of Firth, it didn't look particularly awe-inspiring. Even so, if this was the correct address, Lillian knew this was her best chance of getting help for little Iris.

She led Iris up the steps and knocked on the door. They were guided into a dim waiting room until a familiar woman appeared at the door, her features strict and not particularly forgiving.

"Walter rang—" Lillian began.

"Yes. The rancid maggot informed me that you were coming. Is this the girl?"

"Boy!" Iris corrected despite having been taught not to interrupt. Lillian sighed.

"Can you help me?" She didn't know who else to turn to. Walter was just one more altercation away from rejecting the girl for acting up like this, and, from past experience, Lillian knew that was not going to end well. For the sake of the child's safety, something had to be done, and no one Lillian knew was as resourceful and up to the task as Hosta Craft.

"This way." Hosta directed them up the stairs at the back. "What's her name?"

"Iris."

"Wakefield, I'm assuming?"

"Yes."

She scribbled something onto a piece of paper.

"Date of birth?"

"May fifth, 1869."

"Don't think for a moment I'm doing this out of the goodness of my heart. I was promised compensation in advance."

"I understand."

"What you did was unforgivable."

"I understand." Lillian avoided looking at her. "But for what it's worth, I—"

"Don't bother. Your words are worthless to me. Leave the girl to me, and I will honour our agreement. That's as far as this goes." She opened the door to an office. "I need you to answer a few more questions, but once we're done here, don't contact me. I will send word when I have something to report."

Lillian nodded and ushered Iris into the office. The woman didn't have to forgive her to deliver what she promised. It would be fine. This was the only option that would save Iris from her father's wrath.

I think I might be able to run Justin's and Julian's inputs through the back loop, and that might muffle the feed before it's fed through either way. It doesn't sever the connection, but it should alleviate the problem.

"What about the girl?"

'She' is listed as 'gender undefined' in the system. I'm not sure what that means, but I might be able to shift that over with your help.

"Shift it over?"

Yes. But it requires you to do a memory swipe with the MOP device to remove anything that might trigger 'her' to switch back. The system collects this information automatically, so if she stops believing she's a girl, it doesn't matter what's been inputted into the system before, it will overwrite what's there.

"So rather than try any forceful interventions, we should just make her forget and persuade her until it sticks?" That seemed like a crude tactic, but with her hands already full with the twins, Hosta was not particularly interested in wasting valuable resources on Walter's offspring. "We'll do that and hope for the best. Can you figure out what you need me to do? I'm sending Justin out again today."

It wasn't enough to fix the problem, but sending Justin's consciousness off through dreamside and directing it to go somewhere far off from Julian seemed to interfere with the twins' connection in a mildly beneficial way. As an added bonus, Hosta could sometimes direct Justin to Vincent to get some valuable info on what Vincent was doing, even if the stupid boy had mostly been up to no good in recent years.

All right. Do you need me to help with aiming this time?

"No, Vincent has been staying put for a couple of days. I'll just use the old coordinates."

Let me know if you need anything.

"Sure thing."

"J ames suggested we should try for another baby," Hosta informed the darkness. "I'm not sure if this is the right time considering Justin's condition, but there could be advantages."

What sort of advantages? The darkness seemed to be twirling Hosta's hair based on the slight tugging sensation.

"Well, for one, to keep James off my back about Vincent's treatments, but also, as one more subject to study."

Hosta!

"What?"

We're talking about a human being here! Haven't we discussed this before? They let go of her hair.

"You know how difficult it is to find research subjects. And besides, we can afford both a wetnurse and a nanny. The baby will hardly be ruined by my neglect."

Don't say things like that.

"Does it bother you? Which part? The baby will be taken care of, and who knows, I might find something that could help my boys."

Or you could have another issue on your hands. You can't keep having more kids as if having more could solve your problems.

"It's not like I can tell James no without that also making things difficult for me."

The man does not have your best interest at heart.

"He's my husband. Whether he does or not, does it really matter?" She was not about to relinquish the stability of her current circumstances, even if it meant risking her health for the fourth time to have another baby.

The voice fell silent. Whether upset over the baby or the husband, there was not a peep from them for another year.

December 1895

"Vincent, it's open! Come on in!" a voice could be heard from inside the pharmacy. "Joyful Midwinter!"

"Joyful Midwinter to you as well... Oh dear, what's happened to you?" Vincent commented on the appearance of whoever had come to the door. From where Hosta was standing behind Aurora and Vincent's ward, it was difficult to see what he was referring to.

"An accident... wait— you're the one to talk! What did you do to your hand? Did you take a tumble?" someone said.

"No, there was a fire at the clinic," Vincent replied. "I'll tell you about it later. It's freezing out there." He held the door open, and Hosta was about to follow the others in from the cold when she noticed who Vincent had been talking to.

"It's you!" she exclaimed, although her head could not produce a name. This was one of the men she'd seen up in the attic, covered in blood. He had cleaned himself up, but the fresh bruises were an obvious indication this was the same person and not just someone who looked alike.

"What's she doing here?" He did not sound at all happy to see her, but the feeling was deeply mutual.

"She said someone was out to get her, so we brought her over with us," Vincent explained.

"That was us!" The young man glared at Hosta in an unsettling manner she was certain she had seen somewhere before. "She wanted to erase Julian's memory and use me as a test subject in one of her deranged experiments—who knows why! She's in charge of a Guardian-damned criminal organisation! We almost got ourselves killed trying to stop her and her husband yesterday!"

"What?" Vincent turned to look at Hosta, and now the both of them were eyeing her with some disdain. "When you said 'everything', you don't mean going as far as pestering and poking my brother without his consent to try to further the research?"

Criminal organisation was a bit of an overstatement, even if some of the funding— The two of them were waiting for her to defend herself.

"Well, I don't know! Is he type eight? Does he have something I could use to help the Guardian pick up your corrupt signature?" There was no other reason she could think of why she'd be interested in this 'pestering and poking'.

"Wait." The young man looked perplexed. "You were trying to help him? How do you know Vincent? Why didn't you just tell me you wanted to study me to help Vincent?"

"I don't know, I don't know who you are!" But had Vincent just called this man his brother? Was it Walter and Lilya's child? The one with the 'issue'? Surely not? "People usually respond poorly to my proposals, and trying to find willing research subjects is such a pain..." He was a little on the short and lean side, but that was clearly a young man in a young man's body! However, if they were related, then for sure, the data might prove of interest to her considering the markers were similar among blood relatives... "As for him," Hosta turned back to Vincent, "I think he might be my son. At least, I'm fairly sure that's him, even if he does look disturbingly like his depraved, treacherous rogue of a f—"

"Hold up!" Walter's son cut her short. "You're her? Justin was right! There was one starting with a V!"

Again with the letters. Hosta sighed. It was already exhausting enough to try to keep up with who everyone was and what these conversations were about without the added puzzles. Her head simply could no longer keep up. It was already aching from the effort.

"Look, I don't want to interrupt or ruin your Midwinter," she said and rubbed her temples. "I only came here because Vera said there are some people I should meet, but if I'm not wanted, I'll be on my way."

Walter's son's expression was no longer as hostile, but his intense curiosity was almost as unbearable. It was a struggle to maintain eye contact, but looking away now might look shifty and cause a misunderstanding. She needed to seem human.

"I don't mind having you here, but I think we should ask the others whether they want to share their Eve with you—" The young man's attention was thankfully diverted by the person behind her.

Lilya guided Hosta gently a few steps aside. In the nick of time, too, as the headache seemed to be getting worse, and Hosta could sense the overwhelm looming just overhead if this continued.

Now was not the time to have an episode or to crumble to a heap and cry. That was reserved for other people with legitimate reasons. Hosta couldn't even remember what she had to cry about. And even if she had some reason to, there were other priorities before she could get to that.

Not now, she reminded herself and took a deep breath. She needed to press all that deeper down to not draw more attention to herself.

March 1877

"Where is he?!" Hosta entered James's office after checking the exam room where Julian was supposed to be waiting after returning from school. He'd been suspended for a week for unbecoming conduct towards a fellow student, again. Hosta was yet to get a hold of him to try to talk some sense into him.

Yes, the situation with Justin was only getting worse, and it must have been affecting him. But now more than ever, Hosta needed Julian as calm as possible and out of trouble.

Julian hadn't been in any of his usual hideouts at the clinic, and he certainly wouldn't be at his father's office, but there weren't that many other places he could be.

"He was here about an hour ago." James turned to look up from his work. "I gave him a stern talking to about the trouble he's been causing and told him to behave for his brother's sake."

"How did he take it?"

"Well, he wasn't too happy about it." James sighed. "He wants to see him."

"He can't right now."

"That's what I said, but you know how he is."

It was imperative that Julian did not see Justin in the state Justin was in, even if the two seemed much too aware of each other despite being kept apart. Julian was always in a worse mood if Justin was not doing well regardless of them seeing each other. However, by keeping them apart, the damage so far had been at least somewhat manageable, and Julian seemed to have been in a minutely better headspace.

"Justin can't be exposed to him right now. The situation is too dire. I'm sending Justin back to Schadesborough to the main clinic so I can use the better equipment but also so there's a bit of physical distance between the boys. Hopefully that will be enough... I'll have him stay at the shoe shop. He's been there before, and Mrs Hargrave knows of the procedures."

"All right. When do you want us to leave?" James was always so accommodating when it came to the twins, even though it was clear by his frown that he wasn't pleased about the change in plans. They were supposed to stay in Firth the rest of the year, and it wasn't even April yet.

"Actually, could you take Julian to Grovestead for me for the week he's suspended? Just to keep an eye on him while I make sure Justin is all right. This next treatment will be crucial, and I can't afford anything to go wrong. Grovestead is peaceful." They had a small country house there where Julian would likely not get into any more trouble.

April 1877

Hosta had taken Justin to Schadesborough a week ago. Julian was still missing, but James had decided not to tell her, assuring her everything was all right. Justin's upcoming procedures were too vital to have her lose focus because of Julian. Besides which, any unpleasant news was not going to be helpful considering the pregnancy.

Firth was a big city, so it had taken James a while to confirm that Julian was indeed likely no longer in it. Once Justin's procedures were done, James would have to tell Hosta and launch a more official search effort, but frankly, as much trouble as Julian had caused lately, James was glad to see he'd taken the advice to get lost.

The only real precaution James was willing to make was to ensure the damn boy would not turn up in Schadesborough, or if he did, that he'd be captured and sent to Grovestead on the next train so he did not make more of a mess of things.

But hopefully, for once in his life, Julian had actually listened to his father's advice and gone as far away from them as humanly possible.

August 1877

What a dreadful summer this had turned out to be! It felt like a miracle that it looked like she would be carrying this baby to term considering the amount of stress she'd had to endure.

At least Justin seemed to be doing much better compared to earlier this year. As for Julian, well, the world was not a safe place for a fourteen-year-old with aggression issues, so every day, Hosta was expecting the dreadful news that he, in turn, had been found dead in a ditch.

James had managed to land a few influential clients, so the funding, at least, had been secured for a few more months. With this, they had also been able to hire new staff at the clinic so Hosta could step down to wait for the baby to be born and to take care of them on her own this time.

She wasn't sure this one would turn out any different from the previous three, but she was determined to do her best and be a better mother. She had honed her role, even practised in front of a mirror and with the younger patients at the clinic, to make sure she came off as someone more warm-hearted and caring that wouldn't scare the baby.

She was just about to leave her office at the clinic when her assistant, Ms Figwort, came in with a message.

"He's being brought in now. He was found near your house in Firth two days ago."

"Where are they taking him? Is he all right?" Hosta stood up as quickly as her physique allowed and hurried to the door.

"Exam room five is unoccupied—"

"Julian!" Hosta would have run had she been able to. Even with Ms Figwort helping her, the corridor to the exam rooms felt longer than it ever had. The sight in the room itself was both a relief and a punch to the gut.

Julian was seated in the chair and conscious but hugging one knee, shaking and visibly in pain. Hosta's first instinct was to give him something for it because, judging by the bruises, he'd been hurt in a fight. But when she leaned closer to inspect his injuries, most of the bruising seemed older than a few days, and when she raised his chin and he opened his eyes to look at her, they were watery, and his pupils were almost fully dilated.

"What did you do? What did you take?!" She would have lifted him up and shaken some sense into him had she been able.

"Let me be."

"Where the hell have you been all summer? Who did this to you?!"

"Is Justin all right?" the boy mumbled. "He's better now, right? Can I see him? Please?" He wiped his nose on his sleeve, then stopped and braced himself before vomiting on himself.

"In this state? Are you insane?" Hosta had just enough time to take a step back to avoid being vomited on. Ms Figwort offered her a handkerchief to dab off the few drops on her dress.

"In a few days?" At least he looked too poorly to cause trouble over being denied access.

"Sweetest Guardian, Julian! This is not right. Your father can't see you like this."

It was bad enough that James had found out about Julian stealing and taking laudanum the first time, and now it looked like he'd been doing something similar throughout the summer? James was no Walter, but he would still resort to grave measures for something this bad!

"It helps me control my temper. Justin needs me to stay calm. Far away and as calm as possible..." He closed his eyes and hugged himself, oblivious of the mess.

"Nurse Sorrel, could you get him cleaned up and find him somewhere to sleep that's out of the way of Mr Craft? I'd rather not pull him into this right now. I'd do it myself, but I..." She desperately wanted to find somewhere to sit for one, but also, the smell of the vomit made her want to heave. It really wasn't a good combination.

Nurse Sorrel and two other members of staff in the room helped Julian on his feet.

"Make sure he doesn't ingest anything unsuitable. Do not give him any medication without consulting me. And give him some broth."

At least the boy was alive for now, but he was likely to feel miserable for some time to come.

S ince Julian's return, Justin's condition worsened again, considerably, but because Julian was making so much effort to not lash out or become agitated and seemed to be trying his best to cooperate, Hosta hadn't the heart to send him off to Firth just yet.

It took about a month before Julian was well enough for Hosta to even consider letting him see Justin, and when they saw each other, their meetings were brief and never on consecutive days.

Justin hadn't improved since his latest relapse, but his condition also remained largely unchanged, so Hosta eventually managed to talk Julian into going back to school in Firth, and just in time for the baby to be born, too, so that she could concentrate on him instead of everything else around her. All she wished for was some peace, quiet and stability so she could figure this baby out and find a new routine.

Unfortunately, it only took until the start of December before she was forced to leave baby-Jonathan to the wetnurse, when it became clear Justin could not wait in the sidelines and needed his mother to work day and night to find something that would improve his ever-deteriorating health.

December 1895

"Do you mind if she joins us? She's not here to cause trouble." Walter's son turned to Hosta. "Right?"

"I'm not sure what trouble I could cause you. I don't know who you are. Except, he looks familiar..." She pointed at Julian. "Are you my son? You're Julian, right?" He looked much older than he did within the clearest of her remaining memories, but there was no mistaking the small twitches and tightness around his eyes that betrayed his unpredictable and often explosive irritation.

"Yes. You seem to have retained more of your memories than expected. Do you remember Justin too, or did he slip your mind?" Julian sat up on the sofa.

"Oh, right. There were two of you." For the tiniest fraction of a second, Hosta looked around for a sign of Justin in the room before a sense of dread hit her, and she forced her attention back to Julian.

"Yes, indeed. A spare if you will. It must have been convenient to have one that's expendable," Julian said and glared at her.

"What do you mean?" Hosta frowned, too confused to even deflect properly.

"You don't suppose you recall what you and Father meant to do with Jonathan and Jacob? The two of them have disappeared from the face of the earth. Were they no longer useful to you?"

"Jonathan? Jacob?" Oh, the baby. The two babies. Right, there were more. Something about that part of her life seemed especially patchy and unpleasant to remember.

Justin.

"Did you care about any of us? Or was it always just about the research?!" Julian's anger seemed to be building up, following a familiar pattern. Oh no.

"Have you been drinking?" Hosta looked around to see what he'd drunk to gauge the severity of the situation. "How much?" She asked the other people in the room, but they seemed distressingly nonchalant about it.

"So what if I have?" Julian snarled back at her. "Is it inconvenient for you?"

"Mother?" A girl's faint voice interrupted them. "Julian? What happened? Why are you so upset?" There was a familiar-looking girl coming down the stairs from what must have been the attic.

Julian directed some haphazard hand signs at the girl. Another unpleasant memory uncovered.

"No, I'm not going back upstairs. What's Mother doing here? Will she be staying with us?" She sounded more assertive than how Hosta remembered her.

"No! I will not have her in this house! I—!" Julian's raging brought Hosta back to the more pressing issue. This was not good. He needed to calm down, or else...!

April 1878

"Didn't your mother tell you that you can't see him right now? Don't you remember what happened last year when you almost killed him with your recklessness? Focus on your studies and stop making trouble for us." His father glared at him in that way that always made Julian want to retaliate. This time he fought to keep it in for Justin's sake, no matter how tempted he was to let go.

"Please..." They had placed Justin somewhere out of reach to make sure they stayed separated. Julian had found out the address and tried to write letters, but he hadn't dared to visit out of fear that it might disrupt something important and make things worse. "It's almost our birthday. Can't I visit him for our birthday?"

"Your mother has said no. I am telling you no. Go back to school and finish the term, and we will talk about it later."

Julian had known for a while now that things weren't going to improve. The little he could sense of Justin felt worse with each day. Even their birthday might be too late.

"Please..." Begging was firmly against his nature, but there wasn't much else he could do.

"Possibly, at the end of summer," his father mused. "If he has improved at all."

That would be hopelessly too late. All Julian wanted was to feel that connection properly for one last time. To tell his brother the things that still felt important to share. They really were going to deny him a last goodbye, weren't they? They must have known the end was near...

"I need to see him!" Julian raised his voice but bit his tongue hard to not let it escalate.

"Then stay out of the way so he'll be well enough to see you at the end of the summer!" his father yelled back, clearly out of patience.

Stay away? How far away would he have to go for it to make that much difference? To the edge of the world? Fine!

"Come in," Hosta called from her desk. "Ah, it's you."

Walter had called a week earlier about another round of treatments for their daughter because, while they didn't seem to stick, they had worked for almost a year, and evidently that seemed worth the money in Walter's books.

"I left her with Ms Figwort," the nanny, the current Mrs Wakefield, explained meekly.

"Good." Hosta raised her hand to receive the payment for the summer's upkeep.

"Pardon my intrusion," Mrs Wakefield said, sounding worried. "But is something the matter?"

Hosta looked up from her papers. When wasn't there something these days? But she was not about to open up to the woman who had betrayed her trust so unscrupulously.

"Nothing of concern to you. You may leave. I will contact you when I—" Hosta swallowed in dismay of her voice cracking. Why now? She dropped her pen and searched for something to hold on to. The edge of the desk was an awkward bulky shape; the desktop itself didn't quite feel sturdy enough under her trembling fingers.

"Oh, dear." Mrs Wakefield hurried over to the desk.

"Don't touch me!" Hosta shrieked in panic that her overwhelm was now on display. "Don't interrupt me! I need to—!"

Justin's treatments weren't working. She needed for them to work. Julian was missing again. She had no time or presence of mind to connect with her baby, and this woman dared to waltz in here the third year in a row asking to fix her damn daughter in the most useless manner when even the Guardian didn't think the child was actually a girl.

"Why do you insist on torturing the damn child? What does it matter whether they're a he or a she? Can't you let them figure it out on their own?!" Hosta clamped her mouth shut.

And stop pestering me with it when my boy is about to die!

"I don't care! It's not for me. It's to keep her— to keep them safe!" Mrs Wakefield responded with unexpected vehemence.

"What?" Hosta frowned.

"Walter will kill the child if they're not a girl! He's already tried it before. I can only do so much to keep the peace!"

"Why don't you just take them and leave?" Hosta suggested. The woman stared back at her as if staring at an imbecile, and her silence was loud enough.

There was no leaving Walter. They both knew it well enough from the years of living under the same roof. The only reason Hosta had managed to throw that stinking butt-nugget out of her life was by making sure she seemed more out of her mind than him. By playing up her insanity, Hosta had managed to persuade the man to leave her to escape the curse running in her family. How was this sweet, amiable woman going to persuade Walter to not pursue her if she left?

"He thinks it's a matter of Iris sullying his name if they're not the perfect daughter. I can only guard them for so long... I need this to work. Please..." Mrs Wakefield seemed desperate.

W hat? Why? No! Damn it! The darkness interrupted Hosta mid-research. She'd been falling asleep at her desk so many times recently she was losing count. But there had to be some way to save Justin!

"Are you in here?!" she screamed. She'd been screaming more out of frustration as of late since, after more than a year, she no longer expected an answer. "Why aren't you here?" she cried. "I can't do this alone..."

She'd developed a theory that might have saved at least some of Justin within the Guardian system, but with no access to the system save for the MOP or the other prototype devices that read the Guardian's output during sleep, there was no way of implementing it without the voice's help.

"You said you were going to help me."

I'm sorry.

Hosta straightened up and tried to find where the words had come from.

"You need to help me. You need to reroute the input and output so that it's linked to the dreamside archive! If I can direct Justin's self into the archive, the system might save it there as an active process without realising—!"

The body dying was now inevitable, but if the Guardian didn't register Justin as dead, there was a chance it might keep simulating his consciousness as an active process within the system for as long as the access marker existed and wasn't too corrupted to link to.

I'm not sure I can do that, but I can find out.

"That's fine... Please try..." Hosta fell to her knees. "Please let this conversation be real tomorrow... please... Please let me not be too late."

M ost of the preparations were done, and while the situation was distressing in many ways, surrendering to the process and having something to preoccupy her mind with was keeping Hosta sane for the time being.

Mrs Hargrave was having a chat with Mrs Wakefield downstairs in the shoe shop to sort out the details of Iris staying here in one of the bedrooms to keep her in a more homely environment during her treatment.

From whatever twist of fate, the two of them were related, and Hosta found herself thinking she might have not hired Mrs Hargrave had she known of this before. But the woman was doing a decent job taking care of Justin when Hosta couldn't be here, so firing her now seemed petty.

"How are you feeling?" Hosta asked Justin. He looked back at her and nodded. "Fine?"

The boy nodded again. Good. There was no need for him to suffer through this. Hopefully the drugs were enough to spare him from the worst of the pain.

Hosta had everything at hand for the embalming process. She'd set up the automated system to deliver the soup of ingredients once Justin's consciousness was safe within the Guardian. Although she was responsible for setting everything up, she wasn't sure she could have done this to her own son without it being at least partially automated. She couldn't afford to be sentimental about it. This had to be done just right for it to stand any chance of working.

"Tell me if it hurts," Hosta said and sutured Justin's mouth shut carefully. Then she held his hand and stroked it gently even though it felt performative. It wouldn't be very long now, so he must have been scared. At least he was well sedated and only barely conscious.

The door to the small bedroom opened without warning, and the high-pitched shriek of a child startled Hosta to her feet. She looked at the door and had just enough time to register someone lunging at her holding a knife, but she hadn't enough time to actually assess the situation before she had taken a hold of what was being thrust at her and returned the favour with the small pocket knife always tucked at her waist.

In the chaos of this wild little being's attack, Hosta lost her balance, and, before she even fully realised what she was doing, her pocket knife sunk deep into Iris's abdomen so easily it was almost as if there was nothing there to sink into at all. Blood exited the wound with alarming speed, confirming the blade had more than nicked the skin, and the child cried out in panic.

"Oh, dear... Oh God!" Hosta threw her knife away and pressed the wound. How deep was it? How bad was it? She glanced at Justin behind her. This couldn't be happening. Not right now! But the child was going to die if left untreated. Hosta scooped them up and rushed down the stairs.

"Help me get her to the clinic! Call a carriage! Hurry!"

Mrs Hargrave and Mrs Wakefield both ran outside with her to hail for someone to take them to the Ear.

"Stay with Justin. Please make sure he's comfortable until I get back!" Hosta told Mrs Hargrave as she and the now panicked Mrs Wakefield climbed into the first carriage willing to take them.

A harrowing hour and a half of surgery later, Hosta had stopped the bleeding, repaired as much as her skills and equipment could and stitched up Iris's wound. There were no guarantees of a full recovery, but at least Iris was still promisingly firmly alive for now.

"What happened?!" Mrs Wakefield asked the moment Hosta exited the surgery room into the corridor.

"She charged into the room and tried to stab me."

"And then what? Did she decide to stab herself instead?"

"No." Perhaps there would have been a way to avoid it had she had enough time to consider it, but she really wasn't about to let a child stab herself, and the outcome had been mostly an accident. Mostly.

She'd been carrying her pocket knife ever since she'd been threatened and bullied at school, and she'd made sure she was quick enough to use it in case Walter or anyone else in her life decided to give her trouble. It had seemed like the least she could do to keep herself safe. "I'm sorry. But I did all I could to make it right. She will likely pull through if it doesn't fester—"

"Did you really have to stab my child? Do you hate me that much?!" The woman was clearly in shock from having witnessed something so horrible. Hosta decided it wasn't worth contesting and let her vent.

"It was negligent of me. I can only apologise. I'll make sure your child gets the best of care here, no charge."

"Hosta!" The woman grabbed her by the wrist.

This gross crossing of her boundaries undid all of Hosta's goodwill in an instant.

"That's Mrs Craft to you!" she retorted back and yanked herself free. "Excuse me!"

When Hosta opened the door, the bedroom was silent save for the tick of the timer and the quiet whir of machinery. She'd guessed as much even though she'd hurried back as fast as she could.

Justin lay lifeless in the bed, expression far from peaceful. The automation had done its job uninterrupted, but there was no telling whether the process had been successful.

Because Mrs Hargrave was unfamiliar with medicine, no one here had been capable of honouring Hosta's request to make sure Justin was comfortable. The woman had told Hosta that it had been too disturbing to remain in the same room with him because of the eerie noises he'd made.

Hosta shut off the machines and closed Justin's eyes for the last time. They were already rigid enough to be difficult to close or set neatly. Thankfully, she'd sewn his mouth shut before she'd been interrupted, or this scene might have looked even more grotesque.

Most of the blood had exited without issue. The embalming mixture in the reservoir had all been used by the automated pump. Hosta removed the tubing and tied off the entry points.

She had to aspirate and fill the chest and lower cavities manually, but with no one else present, everything within this room felt sufficiently outside of reality for her to not be forced to think about it too deeply.

After injecting the second solution into the aspirated cavities, she closed the entry points. It was not a perfect job, but it would hopefully be enough to preserve the body for at least a few more years in a state the Guardian might still recognise as human.

But even if Justin still existed in some form somewhere, there was no way to consider this outcome anything but a bitter failure, and, once the numbness subsided, she knew she could no longer postpone her grief.

* * *

The woman was mad. She'd done something horrendous to the poor boy to make him suffer even upon his death. She had even stabbed little Iris, for heaven's sake!

When Mrs Craft left the shoe shop that morning, Mrs Hargrave seized the opportunity to at least save the boy's body from being desecrated.

There wasn't much time, so she yanked off some of the loose floorboards in need of repair and tucked the body in with his favourite blanket. The boy looked slightly more peaceful with his eyes closed, and even though Mrs Hargrave was glad of the suture holding Justin's mouth shut, the thought of Mrs Craft suturing it while the boy was still alive made her want to cry.

She used the old floorboards to not draw attention to what she'd done, but she would call a carpenter to fix them as soon as she'd completely evicted that woman out of her house.

"What did you do with my son?" Hosta roared with fury. "Where is he?!"

"I had him buried where you and your twisted mind can never find him! No child should ever have to go through what you made him go through, and I know you were planning on subjecting him to something worse even after his death!" Mrs Hargrave ranted at her from the bedroom door. "You almost killed my sister's grandchild.

I want you out of this house, and I never want to see your face!" She grabbed Hosta's hand and dropped something into it.

It was the pocket knife still smeared with the child's blood. Hosta dropped it on the floor.

"You imbecile! You buried him?!" Embalmed or not, depending where she'd done it, Justin's body might not withstand it. And how was she supposed to check if his consciousness was safe? According to the voice, it was easiest when within Justin's dreamside range, which by the reports of her research team hadn't been much. What if he was lost in the darkness somewhere, alone? Was he even there? How was she supposed to find him?

"You take your filthy knife and ugly self out of here this instant!" Mrs Hargrave picked up the knife and thrust it back into Hosta's hands. The ornate hilt felt grimy and disgusting against her skin. She wanted to heave.

"You'll regret this." The temptation to smash that woman's face in was great, but Hosta couldn't afford to waste time. She needed to find where Mrs Hargrave had buried Justin as soon as possible. And she needed to find Justin's consciousness before it was too late to apologise to him for leaving him alone. The knife she discarded as soon as she was out the door.

The nothingness had taken away most of the pain, and for a moment, he'd felt euphoric to be released from it. But the longer he spent in this state, the more he realised it wasn't an improvement.

Echoes of his past experiences flashed through his mind, but each time they did, they felt a little weaker. There was a steady background noise from Julian's presence, but it was faint and deeply unsettling, like having to watch someone slowly self-destruct without being able to help.

Ducks. If he could have at least had the ducks to keep him company. Why he'd latched on to the idea of ducks, he wasn't sure, but something about their silly beaks and soft shape was comforting—a beacon of orange and white amidst this darkness.

He couldn't even shout to let someone know he was still here. His mouth refused to move entirely, and his eyelids felt too stiff to open.

I'm here, though.

What a cursed existence.

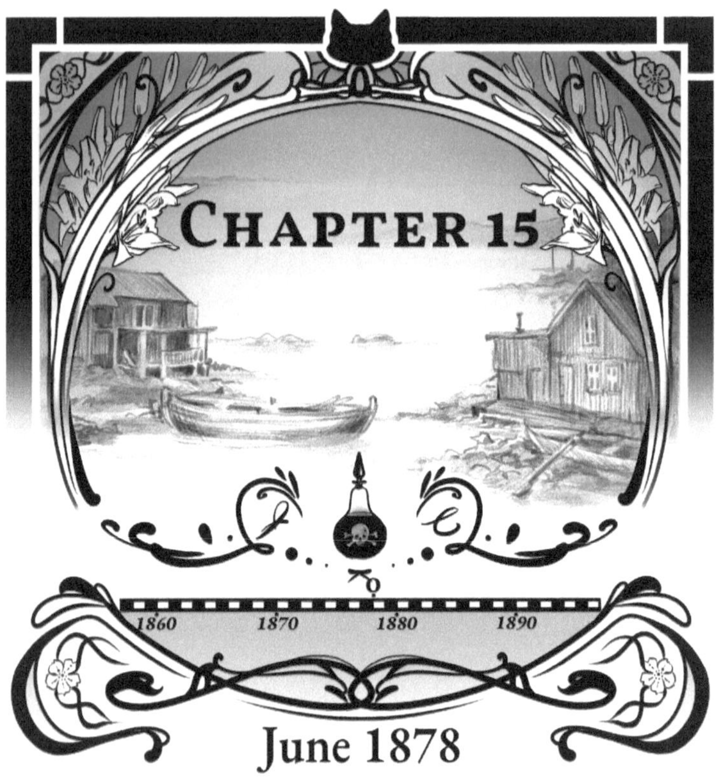

CHAPTER 15

June 1878

Drunk out of his mind, Julian didn't experience much remorse trashing up the local drinking establishment in Herring Cove, and the company he was keeping mainly just laughed at his antics in obscene merriment when they were chased out at gunpoint.

Far from home, the last thing he expected was a lecture from his mother, but that was exactly what he received.

"What do you think you are doing, Julian Craft?!" His mother grabbed him by the collar.

"Where-e 'ell did you come from?" Obviously even Herring Cove wasn't far enough to escape the woman's clutches.

At least Quin was back at the boat and not here to witness this embarrassing spectacle. Julian had fought hard to earn the respect of the company he was keeping, and this would certainly remind them of his inconveniently insufficient age of fifteen. He was just drunk enough to retaliate and push his mother off but not drunk enough to not understand why she was here.

"The real question is what do you think you're doing running off to the edge of the world at a time like this?!"

"Whassit matter?" With how strict he was about maintaining his image, he caught glimpses of some of his groupies watching him in visible dismay. But it had been two weeks since the change in his connection to Justin, and if she was here, it wasn't because the news was good.

Julian started to scream.

He would have liked to believe the reason Justin was gone was because their mother had finally succeeded in severing their connection completely, but despite the drugs and the drinking, the moment before losing Justin had felt too sharp to be his imagination. Something seemed to linger there like a ghost, but it felt like an echo of torture that wouldn't go away no matter how muddled his head became.

Those last moments repeated on a loop, so, if he screamed like a madman, it felt only fitting in the face of this pain.

Perhaps she would kill him if he begged for it loudly enough? Perhaps she was finally mad enough at him to do it and let him go with Justin? He'd failed to go far enough. He'd known there wasn't enough time and that it wouldn't help, but he'd done it anyway. If nothing he did made a difference, then surely he was better off dead. He'd never been anything more than a nuisance in their lives, and now the only person who'd understood him was gone.

Julian became aware that it was only his mother left to witness him coming undone. The others had thankfully retreated, likely disturbed by their young colleague acting more his age.

"He's gone, but I'll be damned if I'll let you go as well!" His mother yelled at him. "You need to stop this idiocy and come home."

"He's still with me…" Julian cradled his head and staggered around the yard. The more he drank, the more it seemed like Justin might still be there. "He's in there. I jus' need to find him…" he slurred, stumbled on his feet and fell down.

Hosta pulled him back up to stand.

"He's dead. It's over. You need to shape up and worry about your own damn self for a change. Do you know how much it has cost me to pay for all the damages in your wake? You need to stop breaking things because your father and I can't afford to mend them!"

"Then don't! Who asked you?" Julian staggered a few steps but fell over again. Ah, he'd done such a good job of ruining himself this time. "Stop tryin' to lift me up. I'm shit." He waved his mother's hand off when she tried to pull him back up again and started laughing.

"Suit yourself."

Julian woke up to someone testing whether he was still breathing.

"Who the f—?" He tried to shoo them off of himself.

"It's me."

"Quin?" At least it wasn't any of the others. At least it wasn't his mother. Maybe that had been a drunken dream?

"The others told me you were making a lot of noise. Do you need help?" Quin kissed his forehead. It never ceased to amaze Julian that he was willing to press his lips on trash as if kissing something worth worship.

"Like I'd need anything from you." He pushed Quin off and scrambled up. "Shit. I feel disappointingly sober. Do you have something to fix that?"

"I have a few things." Quin smiled at him.

"Good. Oh—" The kiss tasted familiar. A distraction to take his mind off of killing himself. Something to make this existence a little less painful. Whatever this was, it was the only thing keeping him afloat, so he clung to it with all he had.

I found him! Lilya announced when she jumped into Hosta's bubble.

"Where? Is he all right?" As per usual, Hosta flailed around blindly until Lilya took her hand and pulled her up to stand.

He's in the system. I don't know where his body is, but he's still there. I'm trying to lead him somewhere where you might be able to access him with the MOP. But the main thing is he's there!

"Oh, thank heavens." Hosta tightened her grip on Lilya's hand to yank her closer and into a hug.

Uh, oh... She tried to escape, but it made Hosta only squeeze her tighter. This damn woman. She'd stabbed Iris, for goodness sakes. She was clearly no defenceless angel, yet she clung onto Lilya like she needed saving.

"Thank you. Thank you so much!" Hosta's seemingly fragile frame shook from the sobs. Damn this woman. Lilya took a deep breath.

Don't thank me yet. I'm not sure whether it can be done, but I'll try—

"As long as he's there," she paused to swallow, "I'll think of a way. I can't—"

Well, by the looks of it, the thing she couldn't do was speak from the crying. Lilya held her close and stroked her hair to try to calm her. It usually helped, but considering the situation, it wasn't a surprise it didn't seem to do much now.

Don't try to speak. It's all right to cry, she reminded her.

Even if Iris seemed like they would pull through, Lilya felt like crying, too. She wanted to hate Hosta for being so cruel and selfish, but the woman had looked almost equally horrified by the situation as she had, and Hosta had always had trouble emoting outside of dreamside. Or maybe Lilya had learned to read her better? In either case and in hindsight, there was no way that could have been anything but an accident.

The woman was already dealing with so much, and ultimately, she'd abandoned her own child to save Lilya's. Calling her cruel and selfish in this context was hardly fair.

"Please stay a little while longer. I don't think I can hold myself together on my own," Hosta whispered.

Don't you have James?

"Like I could trust him..."

Lilya nodded to herself. Anyone moving in so quickly even before the divorce was official seemed suspiciously opportunistic. The man had never appeared particularly trustworthy from what Hosta had talked about him, and clearly she hadn't married him for love or even true companionship. Yet, they did get along much better than she ever had with Walter, so it seemed like she might grow used to him.

Why would I be any better? It wasn't as if she'd been there for Hosta when she'd needed her. Her range wasn't broad enough to reach Firth or the Schades from Dritsby. Grovestead was about as far as she dared before the distance became too disconcerting.

"I don't know. Don't make me think about it too deeply. I want to trust you." She backed from the hug, felt for Lilya's hands and held them while leaning her cheek on where Lilya's heart was. "I can feel it beating. Won't you tell me who you are? Don't tell me it doesn't matter."

I'll tell you, but not right now. Let's get through the grief first while you feel like you can still trust me.

She wanted to tell her, but introducing that shock to her in this vulnerable state was too cruel. Last time she'd tried, Hosta had become so distraught, it had alerted James to wipe her memory of the day. It was a mixed blessing that the man would do this every time Hosta became too upset over something. Usually, Lilya would withdraw the access credentials if James tried to wipe something too substantial, but in this instance, it had seemed like the kinder option. Hosta had enough on her plate without worrying that she'd bared her heart to the woman who had betrayed her trust.

But Lilya couldn't resist kissing Hosta's hair and holding her close for a moment, even if she knew once she found out for good, there would be no future for this relationship. Still, these short, intimate moments had always meant the world to her, and she needed that as much as Hosta seemed to need her.

"A while longer," Hosta whispered.

Take as long as you need.

CHAPTER 16

July 1882

Thank the actual ever-loving deities for James having a handle on the finances. Hosta didn't want to think about the lengths the man had had to stretch to for them to afford the research as well as the staff taking care of Jonathan and Jacob, not to mention the resources going into keeping track of Vincent and Julian.

Vincent had gone back to Whitskersey, and he was less of a burden right now because his condition, while not optimal, had been mostly stable and as good as it could be for the past few years.

Same could not be said for Julian, who had disappeared to one of his habitual, self-destructive summers to who knew where. He'd managed to find a spot so remote, Hosta wondered if he'd left the continent altogether since her network and Justin had been unable to locate him.

This year, he'd resurfaced somewhere beyond the Nishkakar-wat Mountain Range in a town called Nishkawillat, and the only reason she had received word of it was because he'd done something worthy of landing himself in the local newspaper.

The upside was that the newspaper report was about some major acquisitions in mining and not him destroying local property, but knowing Julian's nature, it seemed highly unlikely that he'd actually straightened himself up and gone into any upstanding sort of business. It seemed more like someone had swindled him out of his money with some shady investments.

"The boy is giving me a bad name," James said as he read the article at the breakfast table. Hosta had considered keeping the matter from him, but it would serve as forewarning in case Julian came crawling back in debt, asking for money. "I discussed this only recently with Mr Murray. Dealing with the Nishkans is the same as throwing your money away. Even if the mountains were full of precious minerals, there's no way any of that wealth will ever reach civilised hands."

"At least he's alive." Hosta sighed. James looked up from the newspaper. Sometimes it seemed like he was questioning whether that was a good thing.

"Nishkawillat is far away." He took a sip from his coffee cup and turned the page as if a Nishkan newspaper from a fortnight ago could offer him something more interesting than the article about his son.

Hosta cleared her throat.

James lifted his gaze again, then rubbed the creases forming on his forehead.

"Can't we just enjoy this moment of peace?" he said and took off his glasses. "Don't tell me you want to go fetch him from the other edge of the world?"

"Only the continent," Hosta corrected and put her hand on his. "He is your son. I have developed a few more treatments that might help him. The ARF study has shown a lot of promise, and we're almost done with the preliminary testing."

It was James's turn to sigh.

"If he lays one finger on you, I will let him have it back in a pouch," he warned.

"Don't worry about it. I am hardier than I look."

"I don't care. I see one more bruise on you, and I will return it tenfold, son or not." This part of James always made Hosta a little uneasy, but it was James's way of communicating how important she was to him. She just wished Julian had also been important. "Nishka may be too far this time of year. You might be caught in a snowstorm if winter comes early."

Right. The look in his eyes was enough to tell Hosta this had less to do with the weather and more with James's continuous dislike of letting her out of his sight.

"Perhaps it would be best to try to lure him somewhere closer by so that I don't have to go as far as Nishka myself," Hosta suggested with perhaps unwarranted optimism. James reversed the position of their hands and stroked her thumb with his thumb. "Please... I'm too old to carry more children for you," she reminded him.

"I'm not sure it's safe for you to go." He let go of her hand and looked away.

"How is it any safer if I'm carrying your child? Haven't I already proved to you that you can trust me?"

"Wouldn't it be lovely to have a little girl around the house, though? Surely after all these boys, we're due a little girl."

"James..."

"He wouldn't hit someone carrying a child, would he?"

"I've told you. He's not in his right mind. He can't control it. Especially with his addictions."

"Even so, I really wouldn't mind another child. Wasn't I right about Jacob? Wasn't he just what we needed?"

It was true that Hosta had felt inexplicably lighter around the time of Jacob's arrival, but could that really be attributed to Jacob?

Postpartum had never been particularly easy on her emotionally, even if with Jacob she'd had plenty of help and knew exactly what she needed to do to avoid most of the connective issues her previous children had had. Jonathan had also had the benefit of his mother's understanding of the Guardian, and it seemed like he was developing mostly normally. Both Jonathan and Jacob were so much easier to take care of than their older siblings, it had always felt like cheating. In this respect, if her body could still handle it, a sixth child didn't sound too bad an idea... A girl could prove very beneficial in terms of data.

"We could try..." Hosta supposed. This brought a smile to James's face. "But I cannot promise it will take."

"Leave it to me." He puffed his chest.

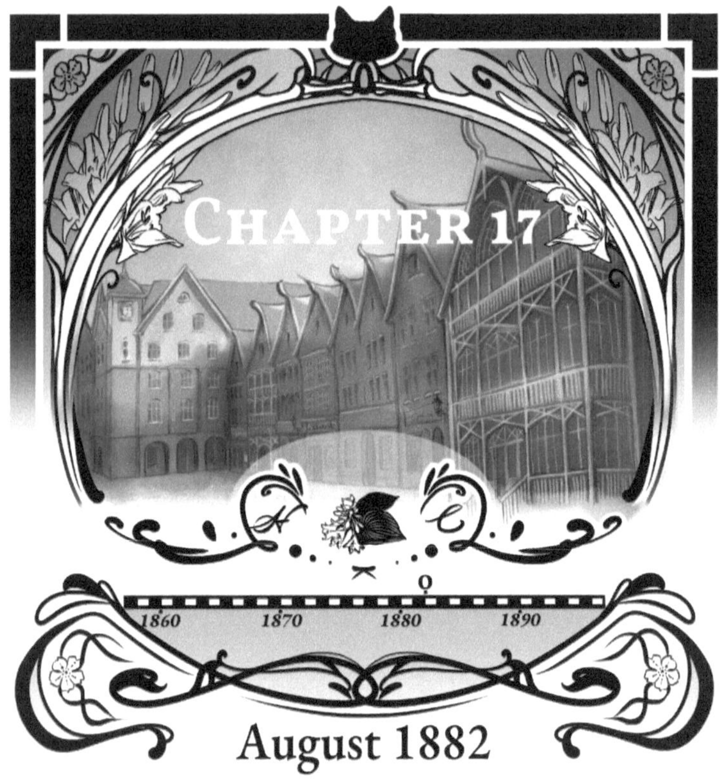

August 1882

As luck had it, Hosta's network reported Julian to be on his way to Firth come August, so while James was still adamant about the matter of another baby, he agreed to them travelling to Firth for a few weeks, as that gave him an opportunity to take care of some of his own business in the area.

Because the Crafts' main residence had been at the Ear of the City in Schadesborough for several years now, it seemed to come as a surprise to Julian that the house in Firth wasn't unoccupied when he stopped by to pick up something he needed.

"Julian," Hosta acknowledged him as he entered the front room. He was wearing a travel-worn coat and some tattered trousers that made him look more like a Northern vagrant than the son of one of the wealthiest, most influential families in Firth. He could have also used a good wash, but no amount of scrubbing would help him be rid of that scowl.

"Mother." His delayed response and drawl revealed he'd been using, but it was difficult to tell whether he'd been drinking or taking other drugs. "I came to get something. I won't bother you for long."

"Where were you?" Hosta asked and positioned herself between him and the door in case he intended to make a run for it. She wouldn't be able to do much to stop him if he wanted to leave, but at least it might delay him and make him hear a few more of her words.

"It doesn't concern you." He seemed to be searching for something from his pockets. "Here." He proceeded to offer her much too large a wad of paper money to be carried around in a coat pocket. "I will pay the rest back later this week."

"I don't want your money."

"Then what do you want?"

"I want you to come home. I want you to stop doing this to yourself. I can help you."

Julian chuckled and set the money on a side table.

"No one can help me." His laugh still bore no genuine mirth. "But don't worry. I won't be sullying your name for much longer." He rubbed the bridge of his nose and wiped his gaunt face with his hand, and, engaged in these habitual fidgets, he was clearly avoiding her eyes. Something about him suggested he was tired of living, and nothing scared Hosta more than the thought he'd already given up.

"You're not sullying my name. And furthermore, I am not your father. I do not care about such things."

Julian looked up at her.

"What do you care about?" He seemed to be asking in earnest but didn't wait long enough for Hosta to form her answer. "Besides Vincent and the research? Besides fixing me because it bothers you to see that I'm broken?"

"Believe what you will, but I don't enjoy watching you suffer."

As with most of Julian's moods, this one, too, seemed to emerge from nothing. In an instant, he had taken her by the throat and slapped her face.

"Baby! Baby!" Hosta shielded herself in haste and tried to retreat from his grasp.

"What? Again?! Wasn't five already enough? Do you mean to populate the whole Realm?" He let go of her, but he was redirecting his explosive anger to some of the surrounding furniture. "Well, if you're about to make more, why can't you let me go?!"

"I already lost Justin!" Watching Julian rage always made Hosta want to join in, throw things and scream, but she bit her teeth and resisted the urge. "I'll be damned before I'm losing you both!"

"I'm leaving!"

"You listen to me, Julian Craft, you piece of shit!" She took him by the collar. "This city is *mine,* and I will not let you leave it on your own." She had a good number of people who would do her bidding, but she wasn't entirely sure whether they'd be enough to detain Julian if he was determined to do away with himself. This bluff had better be effective, or this could be the last chance she had to talk some sense into him. "You are coming home with me to Schadesborough."

"Like hell I will!" Julian was about to push past her.

He wasn't going to give her another chance. This was likely it. Fuelled by desperation, cursing that she couldn't trust James to be there to help her, she gathered all her strength and dealt Julian the hardest slap she could muster.

With some luck on her side, he was too muddled by whatever he'd been taking to have full command of his faculties, so this blow to the ear was enough to throw him off his feet.

"You are coming home with me right this instant, young man!" she growled at him.

Julian stayed put for a moment, leaning to his hands, facing the floor.

"S-stop yelling at me..." he whimpered between some shallow breaths.

He'd been busy playing an adult for years now, but thankfully, at least for now, she'd managed to force him to drop the act.

"You should know I've had a chat with Mrs Quin about you, and she's not best pleased with where you've been dragging her son for so many years! I promised her I would talk some sense into you before you pull someone else down with you!"

"Mrs Quin?" Julian looked up at her, fearful.

"Yes! We know what you've been doing with her son, Adair, for the past, what has it been? Four, five years? If you care about that boy at all, stop being such a selfish ass. Do you know the trouble I've had trying to smooth things over with Mrs Quin? How much worry you've caused her?"

"But I—"

"Don't you understand you're ruining someone else's health with your reckless self-harm!"

"But that's why it needs to end. I need for it to end... I need all of this to end before I hurt him. I have no control over it, and it keeps getting worse!" He raised his voice, but it seemed he was still too dizzy to get up.

Hosta knelt down next to him.

"If you're so willing to throw it all away, then what have you got to lose if you let me help you? All I'm asking is a little bit of trust."

"You don't understand." Julian's face twisted like he might want to vomit. "You're not asking me to trust you. You're asking me to let *him* do whatever he pleases with me."

Hosta frowned, unsure how to respond.

"Ask yourself why you're so fine with all of it. You know what happened to Justin. Why are you so fine?" Julian sat down for a moment, then helped himself back up to his feet with the aid of a table. "Let me go."

"No."

"At least let me go for now. Let me finish this for Quin. I need to make sure he's all right without me…" He staggered towards the door. Hosta grabbed him by the sleeve.

"What will you do?"

"I've set him up with an income. I have a few more meetings with my associates, and the rest should take care of itself. I should be able to pay you back as well. I don't want to leave with debts unpaid…"

"If I let you, will you please, *please* come back to me safe?" Hosta tightened her hold on his sleeve.

"You have my word."

In case his word wasn't worth the shit between the cobble and a horse's hoof, Hosta grabbed a hold of him to hug him tight.

"Please come back to me," she whispered as if bounding him with a spell. "I can't lose you, too."

"I'll let you have my carcass when I'm done with it, I promise."

September 1882

There was no trusting that melodramatic, gaping dunghole! Hosta gritted her teeth and pulled her cloak closer as she ran from the carriage into the downpour. The buggered arse could have picked a nicer weather, at least, for expressing his stupidity!

Guessing Julian hadn't had the foresight to bring anything with him that wasn't already in his ample stash, and, with his habitual use, he'd run out before he was done with whatever he was here for, Hosta had used her connections to cut him off from purchasing anything potentially lethal from the local pharmacists and other suppliers.

Substances barred, the easiest, most popular way permanently out of Firth was the Grand Grymesk Bridge. She'd long since paid for guards to keep an eye on Julian, it and all the other taller bridges or landmarks in the area, and him being so unimaginative and predictable meant that Hosta was already on site by the time the fool even stepped on the bridge.

"You ass! Did you really think I would let you!" she screamed once he'd ambled close enough to likely hear her through the wind and the rain.

He looked up but closed his eyes and looked away.

"Couldn't you just...?" His mumble was barely audible.

Hosta took some steps to pick up some force to her slap. He did nothing to dodge it and stumbled sideways from the impact.

"Liar!" Hosta shoved him. "I said I would help, but you weren't even going to give me the chance! You feeble coward, I hate your guts! I hate you! Why can't you ever do as you're told? Why can't you ever behave? Why are you like this?!" She grabbed the front of his coat to shake him. "You piece of shit! Don't you understand how much I've done for you! Everything I've sacrificed—!"

"Was that ever really for me?" Julian staggered backwards and out of her reach. "I didn't ask for it. I didn't ask you to waste your time on me." His tone was listless and devoid of the spark that would usually so easily send him into rage. Somehow this was worse, and it only fuelled Hosta's ire.

"You are my son! You're my responsibility!"

"More like an obligation. It's all right. Everyone knows the sort I am. No one will blame you for giving up on me. Let's stop with the charades." He would still not look her in the eye.

"You're my son," Hosta repeated, unsure why that bore so much weight she had to say it twice. She'd never quite under-stood why it was significant, just that it was.

Julian looked up.

"So?" He seemed to share her dismay.

"You're my son..." Hosta frowned. Wasn't that supposed to mean something?

"But what difference does it make?"

"I'm not sure I understand..."

"Vincent is your son, but all you do is curse him for running around the continent and making your life difficult. Justin was your son, but you resented having to prioritise his treatments over your research. Jonathan, Jacob... you've made sure they're taken care of, but do you actually care about any of us? I've certainly never been anything more than a burden to you. This way there will be one fewer for you to carry."

"That's not true." It sounded eerily true, though. The miserable young man in front of her was her responsibility. He was a problem she needed to fix. There might have been more to it, but so long as there was an issue to fix, she couldn't quite see past it. It was like her mind refused to rest or let go of fixing it... But why?

Hosta realised she was trembling, and it wasn't because of the rain and the cold. Not fixing it seemed...

"I can't—" she tried explaining it, but something about this was too much for her mind to grasp. "I have to fix it first, to... to... I'll... If it's broken, I'll..." She looked at him. He was so broken. Too broken. "I need to fix it first before I can... Please let me. Please would you let me fix it?" Why did this feel so big and so overwhelming? Why were the tears trying to force their way out now, when the thought of him jumping to his death had only ever elicited anger?

"Then, will you erase it all for me?" Julian asked. "I'm tired of this. You're free to do whatever, just erase it all off. Cut him off from me. Erase me so I'm someone else. I'll come with you if you can do that for me and promise that you'll leave nothing."

"You'll let me? You'll come home?"

"Yes. There's really nothing left for me. But..."

"What?"

"Either you or the stream down there will have to carry me, because I can't—" The dramatic asshole dropped to his knees and fell on his face. Hosta jumped to check he was still breathing and hadn't actually succumbed to some drug he'd managed to get his hands on despite her precautions.

He was still breathing, but his forehead was warmer than expected in this weather.

"I'll fix this. I'll fix it," she told herself. And when she'd fixed it, she'd figure out the rest.

In some awe, Hosta watched the large blond man who seemed to have seen better days interrupt Julian by taking him by the arm. "Sit down before you hurt yourself!" Julian raved at him.

"No." The man was in no shape to be a match for Julian, but that didn't stop him from raising his voice in response. "This is your chance to deal with it! You're feeling something now, right? Don't chase her out the second it catches up with you! If it feels like you can't contain it and you want to break something, you should go downstairs and scream at a wall until it passes, but you deal with it!"

The dainty young man Hosta could recall seeing somewhere raised his hand like an absolute fool. "Can I go downstairs to deal with it with him?"

"You stay out of this! I'm not going anywhere!" Julian turned to roar at his face. This only made the young man smile.

Oh. Wasn't this that clingy vulture that had circled around Julian before? Mrs Quin's son, Adair? But what in the Queen's good Realm were these two clodpates doing? Didn't they know about Julian's issues with controlling his temper? Were they trying to get a rise out of him on purpose? How was this still the sort of company Julian was keeping? Hadn't things improved at all? "Why are you egging him on?"

"Jasmine, dear," Walter's son addressed the girl on the stairs. He instructed her to take Vincent's ward and the cat—there was a cat in that box?!—upstairs and out of harm's way. Then he turned to his mother to chat about the supper preparations as if Julian weren't still raging at Adair with no one helping to keep his uncontrollable anger in check.

"How much did you let him drink? Has he lost his senses completely?" Hosta tried to direct them back to the obvious emergency. What would make Julian calm down the quickest? Laudanum? Paraldehyde? Something else? James would have known what to do, but he wasn't here. Mrs Quin would be devastated if something happened to her son!

Julian grabbed the poor young man's face, and it seemed like he might either be keeping him still to punch him or so he could rip his jaw off.

"It's best to let him blow off some steam when he gets riled up like this. I'll intervene if they start making out," Walter's son said as if chatting about two puppies play-fighting in the park on a sunny day.

"Please don't!" Adair expressed his death wish.

"Then go downstairs with your bloody foreplay!" Walter's son raising his voice made Julian turn to look in an instant and, as if by magic, let go of the face he was holding.

"I'm sorry. Not sure what came over me." He glanced at Hosta nowhere near as angry as before, sighed and sat back down on the sofa. Was he actually controlling it? Was he making an effort without resorting to laudanum?

Mrs Quin's boy sat down next to him and leaned back, fanning his flustered cheeks with his hand like a teenage girl about to swoon in a too-tight corset.

Hosta couldn't fathom how they had just avoided what had seemed like an inevitable blow up. They all looked as if nothing extraordinary had happened, but it took her racing heart a good few minutes to descend from her throat so she could speak again.

"Look, if it helps any, I don't think of anyone as a spare." Anything she could say would sound hollow, but she felt compelled to try. "My memory is hazy, but I know none of you are a spare or extra or expendable. Least of all Justin. I tried to help him. I was getting so close, but I ran out of time." Perhaps in better circumstances there would have been enough time, but she would die before she made the mistake of blaming Julian for any of it again. "I'm sorry... I'm so sorry. I tried to protect you. I didn't know what else to do."

Julian glared at her, but she couldn't sense any of his usual anger bubbling under the surface. When he spoke, his voice was suspiciously level.

"You hooked me to a machine and used me to spy on people across the city for what? For funding?"

This was Justin, wasn't it? It wasn't the first time Justin had pushed through, but it was the first time she'd seen it happen since Julian's memory of him had been fully wiped.

"That was to keep you active so you wouldn't—!" She hurried to explain. Yes, she'd interacted with him when she'd sent him out to check on Vincent or to find Julian, but usually she'd tried to think of interesting and beautiful places Justin had never been able to visit while alive in hopes he could find some enjoyment in them, something that would replace the ugly memory of dying in agony, alone.

Spying on people? That had been for James's dealings, never without a weighty reason, and she'd always tried to make those sessions as short as possible.

Hosta had never been able to communicate any of this to Justin directly because these spells of him popping out briefly usually meant Julian was out of his mind drunk and causing trouble, and so, it had been impossible to know whether her efforts or considerations had been well-received or unwanted.

Overwhelmed by the thought of missing this opportunity yet again, and worse even, Justin being lost forever before she could find the words to apologise to him, her treacherous, no-good body fell to its knees, and she started sobbing. Sobbing! Now of all times, when she needed to seize the chance to communicate with him!

"Wouldn't what? Cause you more grief?" Justin sounded hurt.

He'd clearly misunderstood her intentions, but her head was a frantic mess from the mounting overwhelm, all of her words were always wrong, and her throat felt too taut for speech from the intense need to cry.

"Die off completely!" she forced herself to correct. "I may have an ugly temper, but I'm not a complete monster!" No longer able to swallow her tears, she was grateful for Aurora offering her a handkerchief so she could wipe her eyes and nose. "I remember enough to know I'm far from perfect, but I wouldn't knowingly hurt any of you—"

"You could have at least let me have the duck, for Guardian's sake!"

"I'm sorry, Justin, but you were allergic!" So what if they saw her struggling, bawling her eyes out with snot running from her nose? This needed to be said!

"What did it matter? I was dying anyway!" Justin yelled.

"Well, I didn't know that for sure!" she yelled back but quickly realised everyone in the room was staring at her, and it was probably not because she was openly crying. "They sometimes connect through the Guardian when he's drunk. It's Justin."

Except, by the tortured look on his face, it was no longer Justin.

"Oh, no." Hosta's heart jumped from another fright. James had assured her he'd removed all of it! It shouldn't have made a difference if they got connected since Julian wouldn't be able to remember who Justin was. It should have been like connecting to a stranger! But that look was unmistakable.

Wasn't there any way of shielding him from this? Was it coming from Justin or from the Guardian? Hosta rushed to take him into her arms, all the while knowing how insufficient it was.

"Justin..." Julian wheezed and leaned on her.

"There, there. I'm sorry. It's OK. He's still there." She squeezed him, afraid to let go.

"Don't you try to soothe me, woman!" Julian shrieked but thankfully didn't push her away.

"Do you want me to take away the pain? I'll take away the pain..." She held on to him wishing it could have been as easy as that. "You shouldn't drink, right? It's not good for you."

"Shut up, you hag!" Julian let out some of his anger, but it was frightfully half-hearted. "I should destroy you..."

"I know. I'm sorry." Please don't give up. Please don't sink into that darkness again. She squeezed him tighter for all the times she'd let go too easily.

"Quin...?" Julian looked up from her shoulder.

"He's there," she whispered to him. "See. You took good care of him. He's fine. I know you've tried so hard and done your best. I'm proud of you."

"Why does it still hurt? You promised...!"

"I'm sorry. Life is like that, and it's not very fair. I couldn't lose you."

"It hurts."

"It'll get better. I'll make it get better, I swear."

"I'm sorry. Excuse me," Aurora interrupted them softly. "This seems important, but we're probably all tired and hungry and not in our best frames of mind. Perhaps it might be wise to rest and have a bite to eat before you resume this?" She turned around. "And for heaven's sake, Vincent, sit down!"

Vincent flinched, tottered over to one of the dining chairs and sat down as told. How had he turned out this obedient when the rest of them were so defiant over everything? He couldn't have taken after his father, so was it just Aurora's influence?

"Does it hurt? You'll open the wound on your palm if you keep doing that." Aurora did seem to have a knack for handling him. "Ah, Julian? Would it be possible to get something for his knee?" she requested with enviably smooth ease.

Julian straightened himself up and drew a deep breath. "Of course. I'd hesitate to give him laudanum considering that cough, though." He seemed much taller and sturdier—no longer the gaunt ghost he'd been in the past.

"Camphor liniment, then? Or acetylsalicylic acid?" Aurora asked him.

"Yes, although their efficacy for such severe pain may be limited..." He was conversing almost as if nothing had happened. There was still a hint of melancholy in his voice, but he seemed to be calm—even without it being Justin's influence.

"The food is ready," Lilya said.

Aurora finished spreading the liniment on Vincent's knee, and Julian mixed him a dose of acetylsalicylic acid into a half a glass of water.

And here she was, watching them move on from a situation that had seemed like it should have ended in an outright disaster. Somehow between them they had resolved it. All without her fixing anything. Hosta was glad, but why did she feel so rotten? She was supposed to be happy for them, wasn't she? It seemed like things were fine now.

Were they fine? Were they really? Was it all right for her to feel relieved and relax?

She took a seat at the table as the others gathered around to either also take a seat or stuff food on their plates and eat wherever there was space to sit.

It was difficult to concentrate on what they were saying. Vincent was opening up about something, but Aurora was doing an excellent job at making him feel better. It didn't concern Hosta. Julian seemed subdued next to her, but he kept glancing at both Adair and Lilya's boy with the strangest look in his eyes. What was that—?

"All right, the pair of you," the younger recipient of Julian's obsessive looks disrupted Hosta's thoughts, commenting on Vincent and Aurora. "You're no doubt keeping warm, basking in the warmth of your love, but the food is not as lucky, and it's getting cold." Apparently oblivious that he was also being showered with some obscure type of love, he held up a heavy pot of mash so his mother could reach and add a serving on the plate she was filling.

Once Lilya was done with it, she handed the plate to Vincent and started on the next, but she'd hardly taken one scoop of the mash before she turned back. "Oh, goodness me. I put peas on yours. Should I remove them for you?"

"Huh?" Vincent frowned and looked at the peas. Right. He wouldn't remember something that ancient. He probably hadn't realised who Lilya was.

"Truth be told, I was always most cross that the deceitful maggot took you along with him," Hosta opened her mouth. "Never mind him, but you were so particular with the details and took such good care of my boy, I wish I could have kept you when I threw my husband's foul fundament out the door."

"The peas are fine..." Vincent still seemed confused.

"You have to believe me, none of it was ever up to me." Lilya offered to pour mulled wine into Hosta's glass. "The only reason I asked him if we could take Vincent along was because I was worried you wouldn't have time for him."

"I know. I think I've always known. It's just that the thought of his repulsive face makes me want to break things, sours my mood and ruins my appetite. Let's not talk about it. It's all in the past." Hosta tasted a forkful of the casserole. As she chewed, a strange feeling of recognition crept over her. It wasn't the taste of the casserole, but to make conversation, she said, "This is delicious. Whose is it?"

Lilya pointed at her boy and smiled happily. "It's a family recipe."

Before Hosta could identify what this feeling meant, their conversation was cut short by the sound of the telephone ringing somewhere downstairs.

"I'll get it," Jasmine offered and left the table.

"Who could it be, at this hour on the Eve?" Lilya wondered out loud.

They waited in silence until Jasmine finally returned.

"Who was it?" Julian asked.

Jasmine explained it had been Jonathan and that he and Jacob were up in Grymswich for Midwinter.

"Well, I suppose that puts my mind at ease." Julian emptied his glass of mulled wine. Hosta turned to her own glass.

That meant they were all fine and accounted for save for James, who Hosta had a disturbing, vague memory of seeing with his head cut off. That seemed too gruesome to have actually happened, but if it had...

Hosta emptied her glass.

Her children were fine. That was the main thing. They weren't perfectly fixed or without their respective issues, but they were fine.

Lilya refilled Hosta's glass. Good. Hosta emptied it again. Was it really safe to—?

"Look, I'm going to fill this again, but you should eat." Lilya looked at her sternly while she refilled the glass. There was that feeling again. That was the nanny, right? So it stood to reason she felt familiar.

Hosta concentrated on the food, instead, and, fearing she was heading for another moment of overwhelm, tried to ignore the people around her for a while.

December 1895

After a few more glasses of wine, Justin made another surprise appearance, but this time he was not at all as confrontational as before. Hosta also had the benefit of her swift drinking, so the apologies rolled off her tongue much easier than before.

"I did get you the bloody ducks. There's a whole pond full of them at the—c Clinic." A duck pond was sure to not have burned down in a fire, so the ducks must have survived unscathed.

"How many?" Justin asked, excited.

"There were a dozen to begin with, but I'm sure there are—c now more. Other types of birds, too..."

Justin took Hosta by the hand.

"Thank you." He smiled. It looked peculiar to see that face smiling so happily.

"I'm sorry. It seems I've had a glass too many." This old body couldn't handle them like it used to. "But I really am sorry—c. I'm so sorry. I never meant for any of that to happen. You know that, right?"

His smile disappeared for a brief moment, but it was back when he responded, "I know. I didn't realise before, but I know now. I'm glad you told me. I was so sad. I was so confused. Why would you do that when you said you'd make sure it didn't hurt? But it hurt. And I couldn't understand why you suddenly left... but I think it was to help Rhys here, right?" He waved at Rhys, who looked about as disturbed as Hosta to see Julian's face looking so cheery. He blushed and chuckled, then frowned.

"Am I understanding this correctly?" the young man began awkwardly. "I barged in when you were trying to give Justin a safe send off to preserve his consciousness somewhere dreamside?" He rubbed his frown in some visible mental agony. Poor thing. He'd been much too young to understand what was going on, and it must have looked awful to him.

"There was never any guarantee that it would work, but at that point, it was the only option I could think of to save him." Hosta reached over the table to pat Rhys's hand. "I really didn't mean to hurt you, either." She glanced at Lilya, uneasy. "It was an accident. I even picked up a new blade with a slower opening mechanism just so my fingers can't be faster than my stupid head!"

"If you cut so much as a hair off his head again, I won't forgive you," Julian said coldly.

"Oh, but if I promise never to do that, you'll consider forgiving me?" she asked. He'd always seemed much too resentful to let go of any slights against him.

Julian gave her a sharp look and sighed.

"I've already forgiven you, you old crone. Just keep your hands off of him so I don't have a reason to be angry at you again."

"Really?" Hosta jumped right off her seat to give him a tight squeeze. He made a feeble attempt to evade, but he was much too slow. "Oh, Julian! Do you also want a duck pond? I never thought to ask...!"

"Please don't drink in my presence again, you're scaring me," he requested while trying to gently pry her off of himself.

Rhys burst out laughing.

"What?" Hosta turned to look at him and caught a glimpse of Lilya also trying to hide a smile.

"I'm not Justin. I don't need ducks. I don't need anything from you..." Julian faced away, but he was blushing curiously. Why? Had she embarrassed him somehow? Oh dear.

"I'm sorry. In any case, you will let me know if you want something from me, right? I'm your mother... You know what? I could knit you some socks!"

"You've already knitted me enough socks."

"Mittens?"

"I wear gloves."

"What about for Rhys?" Hosta turned to the young man. "I could knit you a scarf, too!" This made Rhys laugh again.

"I don't know how I didn't see it before, but you're definitely Vincent's mother," Rhys said. "You may not look much alike, but the two of you are just as silly with some drink in you."

"That's not a nice thing to say, dear," Lilya told him off, but she still wasn't doing a great job of hiding her own amusement.

"Can you do the eyebrow thing?" Rhys leaned over the table to ask.

"What eyebrow thing?"

"That! That's it!" Rhys pointed at her and laughed.

"That's it, mister. I'm cutting you off." Lilya moved his wine glass away to the side and gave Hosta an apologetic smile. Rhys humphed at her, then glanced at Hosta.

"I'm sorry. Was that rude of me? It just makes me happy…"

"It makes you happy?" Hosta frowned. "What makes you happy?"

"That right there!" He pointed at the eyebrows again. "And you know, I'm relieved that you didn't turn out to be as evil and scary as I thought you were."

"Rhys!" Lilya gave him a stern look, which he promptly shook off.

"It's fine. I'm not a great person. It's an easy mistake to make." Hosta took another sip of wine. They were tolerating her, and Julian had said he'd forgiven her. That was worth raising a toast for, so she moved Rhys's glass back over and gestured for him to take it. "Here's to me not being entirely evil, even if I am an old crone and a hag." She glanced at Julian and urged him to join in. Julian toasted with her, although reluctantly.

"You're pretty decent," he mumbled very, very quietly and emptied his glass. This and the toast of mulled wine made Hosta feel all warm inside.

"I could knit you a sweater!" She turned back to Rhys. "You look too scrawny to stay warm in the winter."

This made him squint at her with annoyance, but only for a moment.

"Can you also knit him a matching one?" This time Rhys stood up and pointed at Julian. "And one for Quin and for Victor! And Vincent and Vera, and—c" He stopped at the hiccup and looked surprised.

"Sit down, dear," Lilya told him gently.

"I'm not scrawny."

"You're not scrawny, dear. You're drunk."

"That I am." Rhys giggled. "When did that happen—c?"

"When you started drinking, dear. That's what happens," Lilya explained to him patiently. Then she looked at Hosta a little quizzically. "Don't encourage him, love. He drinks too much for his own good."

"Oh, yes. Pardon me." Hosta felt like she must have also had a little too much because she could have sworn Lilya had just called her 'love' in a way that hadn't even sounded out of place.

"Hosta." A familiar soft voice.

"Uh, did I fall asleep?"

It hadn't sounded quite the same.

"No, but you look like you might at any minute. Maybe you should go to bed? Mr Quin said it was all right for you to use his room upstairs, so I've made the bed."

Hosta looked up at Lilya, admittedly groggy from all the food and drink. Julian and Rhys were no longer at the table. When had they left? It was just Lilya there sitting across from her.

"I think it was the wine that went to my head."

"Yes." Lilya nodded.

"I'm sorry. Was it embarrassing?"

"It was fine. They're all tipsy themselves. Vincent fell asleep."

"He did?" Hosta spun around to see. Vincent was indeed asleep on the sofa. "How much? Did Aurora—? Was it—?"

"On his own." Lilya smiled.

Hosta stared at her, unable to think, speak or even move. She was just about to finally shut down and curl into herself for good when Lilya took her by the hand and pulled her along, away from the table and down the stairs.

Once down in the dimly lit back room amidst the organised chaos of Julian's things, scents of chemicals and herbs and the hint of smoke from the log burner, Lilya stopped and gave Hosta a hug. "Cry," she said. "It's not the dreamside, but there's no one else watching."

"Well, I can't cry on command!" Hosta objected, but the tears were already pooling from her eyes. "Shit..."

"It's all right. I'm here." Lilya stroked her hair, and it was impossible not to recognise her touch, her scent and the pattern of her steady breathing.

"So you are." Hosta blushed. This woman had seen her cry so many times that one more shouldn't have made a difference, but this time Hosta could see her gentle expression as she did it.

"Do you think we might be past the grief soon, love?" Lilya whispered. "I don't know how much longer I can bear waiting."

"You should have told me. You should have said something." Maybe not right at the point of the divorce when she'd been at her angriest, but sometime between now and then...

"I did. I told you everything when you pestered me for it, but then James would always give you a clean slate if something during the day had upset you enough. I made sure he couldn't touch any of the important stuff, but there were times I agreed and let him." Her brow furled as she spoke. "I'm sorry. It was not my place to meddle, but I couldn't watch you try to shoulder all of it for everyone else. You had enough to worry about. Are you still sad to see it's me?"

"No. And I doubt I was sad before. It takes me a while to know how I feel even in the best of circumstances. If I was given less than a day to mull it over, I was probably just overwhelmed." Hosta pulled Lilya closer, intrigued by her subtly shifting expressions. She'd never heard her specific tone of voice or seen her face in this context, but she could feel her there, familiar, supportive and holding her up as always. "I knew I should have kept you when I threw Walter's ass out the door."

"I would have preferred that, but he threatened to kill you."

"We could have handled him. Hell, you could have probably handled him on your own based on today."

"I'm not that brave. And you were busy with Vincent. I agreed he was the priority. If you'd let Vincent go with Walter, I might have done something different, but I knew for you to learn to love your baby, you needed to do it your way. You needed that space to figure it out."

"Those are some big expectations for someone like me." Hosta sighed. Was she even capable of love?

"I know what I saw. What I'm seeing now. I see you." Her voice was tender and kind, but Hosta couldn't help but feel nervous.

"And is it any good?" She held her breath.

"It's more than good, my love. It has always been more than good." Lilya leaned in to kiss her. Relieved beyond measure, Hosta lifted the woman up in the air and kissed her back.

"Oh, oh dear!" Lilya looked horrified by her feet no longer touching the ground. "Love, love! Please let me down! Oh—"

Hosta sealed her mouth with another kiss but let her back down. She looked wholly red in the face whilst finding her feet.

"I imagined you'd be taller and heavier..." Hosta said and tried to recall the shape. The few times they'd kissed, she'd always had to face upwards to do it.

"That's because I am when I have the choice." Lilya giggled. "Also, I didn't want you to immediately guess it was me. It was embarrassing enough to have a crush on the lady of the house. I would have died of shame if you'd found out. And how shallow am I to have felt that way even before I got to know you?"

"You were attracted to me for my looks?" This took Hosta by surprise. She wouldn't go as far as feign ignorance when it came to her features, but she'd always considered Walter and James a little dumb in the head for falling for her.

"Well, initially."

"Right. You'd have to make considerable effort to sustain interest in a wrinkly old hag like me—"

"Shush now!" Lilya pressed her fingers on Hosta's lips. "Not that it's that important to me anymore, but you are plenty attractive to me even now."

Hosta gave her a pleased grin and opened her mouth enough for those fingers to slip in. Still grinning, she bit them gently.

Lilya lifted her eyebrows but responded with a smile. "The house might be crowded tonight, but I know a place dreamside that should be quiet enough," she said.

I'm here, Lilya announced her arrival as she stepped into Hosta's bubble. "I mean, I'm here."

Hosta turned her head towards her but didn't hurry to straighten up like she usually did.

"Is everything all right?" Lilya knelt in front of her and took her hand.

"Yes, but I am a little nervous."

The space did feel different from usual, but nervous wasn't quite the first word in Lilya's mind. It was somewhat disorienting, but perhaps it had something to do with the state of Hosta's memories—

"I was a little nervous, so I had a nightcap 'fore bed and din't realise that'd follow me here... I feel a teensy bit fumbled in the head. I'm sorry." Her eyes did seem droopier than usual, but that could have easily been because it had been such a long day.

"Don't worry about it, dear. We don't have to do anything specific tonight. It's been a long day for the both of us."

The feedback from the diagnostic function didn't seem too muddled, but there was a nice relaxed feel to it, so Lilya didn't bother turning it off.

"Can you give me a massage like you used to?" Hosta offered her head by slouching forward.

Bah, what wrinkly old hag...? She always looked the exact same age here, barely twenty. Clearly an adult but young enough to look vulnerable without her usual veneer of confidence and jadedness from her years of struggles. Either was fine, but this sight always made Lilya feel protective like she wanted to shield and hide her from the world.

Lilya slid her fingers through the silky, dark hair and rubbed the scalp carefully until Hosta let out her usual soft groans.

These sounds were such sweet rewards for such little labour, Lilya could have spent hours just listening to them. And the woman seemed oblivious of the power she had over Lilya.

Lilya moved her fingers lower towards the jawline and chin and lifted Hosta's face back up from her slouch to give her a kiss.

"I knew it was upwards," she mumbled, and it was as if she were looking Lilya straight in the eyes despite being unable to see. Her dark eyes gleamed with a few soft, thin yellow lines—a sign of the strange glitch that was likely causing her blindness. She closed them and lifted her arms over Lilya's shoulders to hang from her like a necklace.

Amused by the shameless clinginess, Lilya lowered her down to her back where she spread her arms wide, thoroughly relaxed and unconcerned. The sight of her in this state made Lilya forget herself just watching for a moment.

She sat next to Hosta, leaning sideways over her body, and moved a few strands of hair from her face.

There was still some tightness around the jaw, so Lilya massaged the sides of Hosta's face and neck to relieve it. The thin shift Hosta was wearing was smooth to the touch, but Lilya opened its few buttons and pulled the collar aside to massage around the clavicles. From a moment's impulse, she pressed a few soft kisses on the exposed skin and watched how her breath made Hosta shiver with tiny goosebumps.

What else could she do to make this more enjoyable? There were so many options she was tempted to try if Hosta was willing to let her.

"Do you mind if I—?" She slipped her hand under the shift to feel the skin underneath. Hosta let out a tiny grunt but lay under her touch without squirming. Her breathing became more audible when Lilya circled her breast and nudged her nipple with her fingertips, though.

"I'm sorry... I'm a little useless..." Hosta slurred, mostly from being so relaxed and tired. She tried to reach out for Lilya without much success.

"Don't worry about it, love. In fact, just enjoy how it feels." Lilya guided those wandering hands back down and resumed what she was doing under Hosta's shift. The nipples had perked up, and it seemed like her whole frame had curved just slightly to meet Lilya's touch, so she ran her full palms across Hosta's body to see how she would respond.

"Ahh..." Hosta closed her eyes and crossed her legs, slowly, as if trying to rub something. Lilya placed her hand on Hosta's abdomen and lower down where it was more obvious that she was contracting her muscles.

"You seem to be in the mood for a little more than a massage." Lilya rubbed her mound softly, meaning to ease the tension a little, but it made Hosta make a few more delicious sounds as her breathing grew heated.

For a moment, Lilya was gripped by a bout of jealousy, wondering if Hosta's responsiveness was the reason James had wanted to make so many babies with her. After all, if this was how she was in bed, so easy to please and receptive to every touch, then who could fault the man? The thought was sickening even if Lilya could relate.

Even the soles of Hosta's feet were delicate, and instead of making her ticklish, touching and rubbing them made her moan quietly.

"Lilya..."

Oh, how sweet it was to hear her call her name with such soothing timing! Lilya swept her fingers across her inner thighs to where she was warmest.

"Ahh! Lily—ahhh..."

"How does it feel?"

"Ah, I don't know how to—ah, describe it."

"Try for me, love. I'd like to hear you." Lilya slid her thumb over the labia so that they parted a little.

"Ah, I—" Hosta paused to catch her breath. There wasn't much Lilya needed to do to make her lose her trail of thought. Just fingering the spots Lilya enjoyed herself on occasion seemed to be doing the trick remarkably well.

"I want, ah—" she tried again without much success.

"More, my love?"

"Yes. Ah, that's good. That's, ah!" Her whole body nudged when Lilya pushed just one finger in and pulled it out. To make sure it wasn't just a fluke, she tried it again, and sure enough, a quick slide in and out produced a nudge but also a surprised inhale. "How?"

"What do you mean 'how?'" Lilya chuckled. She pulled up the shift and sunk her face in, lips, mouth and tongue savouring the taste, texture and warmth. Hosta's voice was so beautiful when she could not curb her low, soft moans and heavy breathing. Hearing it made Lilya's insides froth and swirl, and her knees felt weak and her cheeks flushed, hot.

Damn, that woman was so intoxicating without so much as trying! Having to listen to those moans made Lilya feel as if she was the one who had been drinking. It was like someone kept fanning the flames with each soft groan and draw of breath.

"Ahhnnn—!" She was forced to lift her mouth from its prize to breathe and to sober up.

"Lilyah?" Hosta sounded worried.

"Ah, ah... Don't worry..." Lilya backed away to sit, looked up and cooled her face with her forearm. "I'm, ah, I'm fine."

"What happened?"

"Ah, nothing..." Maybe it was best to filter out the diagnostics feedback after all?

"Are you all right? Why'd you stop?"

"I'm fine. I just needed to, ah, catch my breath." Lilya moved the outer labia carefully aside to dip her tongue back in, but as soon as she did so, the feeling was back. She tried to ignore it but yearned to touch herself, which was troublesome because she was technically already touching herself while touching Hosta.

How embarrassing to feel like this from making her feel like this!

"Ahh!" Hosta grabbed her by the hair. "It feels so nice!"

"I—I know..." It was soft and wet on her face and mouth, but also between her legs where it felt almost distressing because nothing was actually touching her, but it felt like something might soon start dripping down her thigh.

"Don't stop," Hosta said, voice consisting of mere breathy wails.

In that moment, Lilya could no longer keep herself from making sounds, too, as it felt as if someone was now teasing her nipples. When she looked up, she saw Hosta absent-mindedly fingering herself roughly where the sensation persisted. She quickly closed her eyes, but the feeling was only compounded by her lack of focus on anything that could have distracted her.

"Hnnh." She was forced to stop again. She hovered there on her hands and knees, her eyes closed, as if up-the-pole drunk from feeling so aroused and steeped in pleasure.

"Are you sure you're all right?" Hosta asked again.

"It feels so *nice*," she heard herself mirror the woman's words.

"It does? Oh—ahhh!"

Lilya dove back in, no longer caring whether it was embarrassing. She dug her fingers in, and it was laughably easy to gauge where to rub and how hard to push and tug because each movement made her throb inside so vividly it left her craving for more.

Thank the Guardian, Hosta could not see her in this state: drooling and breathing on her beautiful, supple body like a heated animal!

She scooped the juices with her tongue and persistently nudged and suckled on the sweet spot until her body finally succumbed to the orgasm and the waves of pleasure flowed through her body, disrupting her senses completely.

"Ah, Lilya?" Hosta called her from her pleasurable stupor.

"What is it, my love?" She tried to coax herself out of this state, but it lingered, making her reluctant to move.

"Did you just—?"

What? Had it only been her? Lilya felt chills down her neck.

"I might have!" Paska! Had it somehow not been as good for Hosta? Was there an error in the diagnostic output? She needed to check the data—

"Oh, good. Ah... So it wasn' jus' me." The drunken drawl was back as she relaxed. "Ah, that was amazin'. I need you to do that again sometime."

"Really?"

"Yeah. 'D you like that?"

"Yes." Lilya crawled closer and lay down next to Hosta, exhausted.

Hosta was smiling with her eyes closed but lips ever so slightly apart while she still breathed heavy breaths. Lilya set her hand on the woman's slender waist and watched her smile, until only a moment later, her lips started to quiver and she nudged from a sob she'd tried to stifle.

"What is it?" Alarmed, Lilya pulled her closer and stroked her cheek.

"I-I'm just happy..." She looked like she was trying to smile as she said it but seemed too overwhelmed to succeed. "It's frightening..."

"Oh, love." Lilya squeezed her cheeks and kissed her. "It's all right. I'll keep you safe."

"Is it really all right? I can't take it if—" She swallowed. "You'll let me know if anything's wrong? You'll let me know before you leave? You promise you won't leave me without a warning? You'll tell me if you're too broken to go on so I can fix you? I can't—" She sobbed.

"I won't leave you, love."

"Promise me you won't leave me!"

"I promise."

"I love you." She could barely get it out from her crying. "I love you. I'll fix you if you're broken, so please don't leave me."

Lilya's heart hurt. It sounded a lot like a drunken ramble, but knowing the person behind those teary eyes staring desperately into nothingness, trying to see her there, Lilya could tell what this was about.

"Oh, love. I can't say death won't ever come between us, but I will never let it do that without a fight, and I promise, if it's up to me, that I will never leave you without warning again." She directed Hosta's eyes towards herself. "Your love is safe with me. I'll cherish it."

Hosta's face twisted into a silly, sobby smile as she struggled to keep herself together.

"I love you, Lilya."

"You are so precious to me, love. You don't even know..." Lilya squeezed her tight, tempted to join in the crying. "I love you, too."

Glossary

May contain spoilers!

Access Marker, an identifier that handles access rights to the Guardian system and its servers.

Ancestors, the people who were in charge of maintaining the Guardian in the past.

ARF mask, the, (the Automated Rest Facilitator), a mask applied to a person to stop them from sleep-roaming and interfering with the Guardian's automated rest procedures.

Credentials, something which grants access to the different functions of the Guardian.

Crook of the Ear, the, a region named after its location on the cat-shaped continent of Furuyan.

Diagnostic Function, a feature of the Guardian that allows the diagnostician to experience the patient's emotional state and sensory experiences within dreamside as if they were their own in order to more accurately diagnose ailments in cases where the patient is unable to process and/or express what they are experiencing.

Documentation, written materials of instruction for system operations, procedures, configurations, and setups for, in this case, the Guardian system.

Dreamside, a diagnostic state provided by the Guardian during sleep.

Ear of the City, the, an affluent area of Schadesborough with a distinct style in architecture and a lot of immigrants from the North.

Furuyan, the name of the continent where this story takes place.

GateKeeper Module, the plugin responsible for monitoring the patients' connections to the Guardian's servers.

Grand Grymesk Bridge, a tall bridge over the Grymesk River in Firth.

Great Grove Bridge, a bridge in Grovestead.

Guardian, the, supposedly a widely worshipped deity on Furuyan, second only to the god of another monotheist religion similar to Christianity. More accurately, an apparatus used for analysing, diagnosing, preventing and curing health issues related to, or through, sleep.

Herring Cove, a place at the Crook of the Ear (see map).

Laudanum, a tincture of opium for pain relief and other ailments.

MOP (Manual Override Panel), a machine used to manually connect a patient to the Guardian for diagnosis or to administer various treatments such as memory manipulation.

Paraldehyde, a central nervous system depressant (with anticonvulsant, hypnotic and sedative properties).

Paska, lit. shit (Finnish).

Whitskersey, the Island of the White Skerries, a small island in the Arctic, near the Crook of the Ear.

Äiyä, Akka and the Lowest Earthenfolk, a swear inspired by Finnish Folklore.

CAST OF CHARACTERS

(with drunk Hosta)

Aelia, Hosta (Wakefield, Craft) A highly determined, devoted scientist and the saintly mother of six incredibly annoying and troublesome children.

Chatbury, Mr A trusty member of staff at the scientists' accommodations in the Ear. Seems too decent to not be shifty. Probably has an illegitimate child with Nurse Sorrel.

Craft, Jacob Hosta and James's fourth child. The little ungrateful brat that only listens to his brother Jonathan.

Craft, James Hosta's second husband. Unsure if decent or creepy? Probably no good.

Craft, Jasmine Hosta and James's fifth child. A sweet girl. Nothing bad to say about her.

Craft, Jonathan Hosta and James's third child. Troublemaker but not as bad as his older brothers. Needs constant adult supervision.

Craft, Julian Hosta and James's second child. A melodramatic asshole that never does what he's supposed to!

Craft, Justin Hosta and James's first child. Not as bad as his twin brother but likes ducks. Who the hell likes ducks?!

Figwort, Ms Hosta's assistant. A total pushover. Boring.

Hargrave, Mrs Stole my baby!!! BURN HER AT THE STAKE!!!

Matron, of the workhouse Another scheming baby thief! We don't even care what your name is.

Murray, Mr James's bodyguard. An old family friend. Daft bugger.

Quin, Adair That clingy vulture that circled around Julian before. Mrs Quin's son.

Quin, Mrs An incredibly lovely lady you don't want to disappoint or make angry. Don't be late for tea because she has likely baked scones and timed it to the minute so they're nice and fresh when you arrive. Being late will hurt her feelings although she will be too kind to say anything about it. She will send you home with a slice of cake.

Sorrel, Nurse Look, I don't remember who all my underlings are. She's a nurse. She's not done anything memorable. If she's a criminal mastermind, she's good at covering her tracks.

Swifty, Ren Vincent's ward. Not his kid. This still baffles me. Who in their right mind would take care of a kid that's not theirs? Ohhhh, right.

Swifty, Vincent Hosta and Walter's first child. A noisy, bitey, clingy, drooly thing that reveals people's secrets and makes them uncomfortable. Darling baby boy. Mama loves you!

Unenhalti, Lilya (Lillian Underhall/Wakefield) The treacherous hussy that stole Hosta's first husband, but she's all right, I guess. Nice upper body strength, handy with a big torch. Yeah, she's fine.

Vesper, Dr (Aurora, Vera, Copper Curls) A rather plain-looking, boring girl that Vincent seems to adore. She's a quick study and not an entirely bad scientist, but I find her suspicious out of principle.

Wakefield, Iris (Rhys) The wild little stabby creature that interrupts important situations! Also, RUDE when drunk. But he makes my boy Julian happy, so let's knit him a scarf.

Wakefield, Walter A cheating maggot.

ABOUT THE AUTHOR

J.B. Thwaite is the author of dozens of best-selling books that only exist in her dreams. She lives in the darkest, most inhospitable depths of Southern Finland with her spouse, scion and feline companion. She has discovered fire and re-invented the wheel in exactly the same form as before but better. With an incredibly busy schedule, she uses her scarce free time to nap, sleep and doomscroll on social media. She is also a connoisseur of the highest quality Asian homo-erotic literature and a bit too neurodivergent to enjoy long walks on the beach.

Also by

The Catnap Ramblers:
Vincent and the Cat (2023)
Rhys and the Voiceless (2023)
Aurora and the Guardian (2023)
The Catnap Fumblers (extra novellas):
Private Afterwords (2024)
Solicitous Missteps (2024)
Feudal Fisticuffs (2024/2025)

Other books in the works:
Pandion (2024)

www.ingramcontent.com/pod-product-compliance
Lightning Source LLC
Chambersburg PA
CBHW061445150726
47987CB00001B/343